DESTINATION ELSEWHERE

Anthology of Award-winning Short Stories

ISBN-10: 0-9742652-6-8
ISBN-13: 978-0-9742652-6-1

DEDICATION

This anthology is dedicated to those who
know where Elsewhere is

To the authors featured in this book: Scribes Valley thanks you for
your time, patience, trust, and talent.
.

CONTENTS

NEXT STOP: ELSEWHERE
A Foreword by David L. Repsher, editor

Greetings and thank you for coming along on our journey of a lifetime to the little-known place called Elsewhere. We'll be leaving soon, so please have a seat and relax. We don't stand on formalities here, so kick off your shoes and let your hair down if you'd like.

Our ride should be smooth and event-free—most trips of the mind are. The actual travel time to Elsewhere will be very short, but please feel free to enjoy the scenery as we travel along, keeping in mind that the scenery is unique and different for every viewer. Not one of us will see the same thing—or in the same way—as anyone else.

But that's what makes trips like this so enjoyable.

If you have decided to bring refreshments, please feel free to enjoy them at your leisure.

Okay, let's see... Yes, I'm getting a signal from the leader of our excursion that all is ready. This is it. Please prepare yourself to be swept away.

Now, take a deep breath, reach down, and turn the page...

FIRST PLACE

ADVENTURE IN THE CAUCASUS
©2008 by Bill Westhead

At age twenty-five, Ed Winder was already an experienced climber, having honed his skills rock climbing in the English Lake District and conquering many Swiss Alpine peaks.

Now, in the early spring of 1910, he sat on the edge of the boulder-strewn valley that lay between him and the mountain and, for the first time, gazed at C10, one of many unclimbed peaks in the Caucasian range.

The mountain seemed to stare back at him, brooding and threatening; a huge hulk, towering over its siblings and rising like a leviathan out of the melee of granite boulders and glaciers that surrounded its massive base. At just over 16,000 feet, its peak pierced the dark, windswept clouds like a finger pointing the way to distant heavens. Rocky shoulders, softened under a mantle of late winter snow, jutted out on either side, then fell away sharply to blend once more with the rocks and ice below. For a million days and nights, storms had hurled their fury at its craggy face, in places weathering it to glass-like smoothness. The mountain's very silence seemed to challenge any man worthy of the name.

Ed had spent two months trekking across Europe by boat and train. Finally, after two days on a particularly uncomfortable Tartar saddle, he arrived in the primitive Russian hamlet of

Minskia, a mere two miles from the base of C10. Here, he found lodgings with Alexei Federov and his wife.

Alexei, a local mountain guide, shook his head in disbelief when Ed explained the reason for his visit. "Cannot climb mountain. Face too smooth. Lot of hangovers and weather suddenly very bad. I know. I try," he said in his best English, a note of contempt in his voice.

"You mean *overhangs*?" Ed said, a smile creasing his tanned face.

Alexei glared. "Go look yourself. You see I right."

But Ed would not be deterred. Day after day, during the summer months of 1910, he reconnoitered the massive peak from every side and, on returning to his lodgings, discussed his findings with Alexei. After several weeks, based on his own survey and Alexei's experience, Ed had ruled out any attempt by either the North or East faces, due to long stretches of smooth, almost vertical rock and several severe overhangs which, Alexei claimed, were impossible to tackle head on and there was no way to go around them.

Ed thought the North/West ridge was promising until Alexei pointed out the dangers of the initial glacier, gale force winds that constantly raked the ridge, the deep snow drifts on either side, not to mention the ever-present unclimbable rock faces.

These obstacles, coupled with the climber being exposed to sudden changes in the weather, would, in Alexei's opinion, make the approach treacherous, if not suicidal.

Finally, by the end of August, Ed had concluded the only way was by the South face. Alexei merely smiled at this conclusion and continued adamant in his refusal to be involved, claiming the sheer, smooth rock faces would foil any attempt, no matter which route was selected.

"We could use pitons and ropes, like the Germans use, on those difficult places," Ed argued.

"Ugh! Germans cheat mountain with spikes," Alexei said. There was no doubting his disgust at Ed's suggestion. "I not cheat. Let mountain win."

By the end of the summer a frustrated Ed Winder returned to England, taking his survey notes and sketches with him. During the winter months he studied his data and finally determined that, despite his initial conclusions and Alexei's warning, the most promising route up the mountain was via the North/West Ridge. He discussed his findings with two close friends, Mark Hardman and Ken Phelps who, along with him, were experienced climbers and members of the famed Alpine Club.

Finally, the three men decided to return to the area in the spring of 1911 and attempt an ascent of C10 by the proposed route. Immediately, Ed wrote Alexei and told him of their decision, their proposed arrival date and requested he find accommodation for the party.

Arriving in Minskia in April 1911, Ed was surprised to be greeted by Alexei's wife, Sasha, who spoke no English.

"Alexei?" Ed asked.

Sasha shook her head. Then referring to a piece of paper said, "Room?"

Ed nodded and held up three fingers. Sasha shook her head again and held up two before holding up one finger and adding, "Egor Popov." From this Ed gathered two of the team would stay at Alexei's home and one with Egor Popov.

Having settled the question of accommodation, he next tried to find out where Alexei was and when he would return. After much head shaking and hand waving, he understood the guide was a long way away and would not return for several weeks.

Annoyed, Ed cursed himself for telling Alexei of the planned attempt on C10 and expecting him to be a part of the team. Clearly, the guide had taken his present trip to avoid being involved.

Determined not to lose time, Ed scoured the surrounding villages for another guide willing to accompany the expedition. It took three weeks before he found the Kosloff brothers, Boris and Lev, two guides eager for the opportunity to join the party. But there was a snag. The brothers had already been retained for the next month by David Barnes, a twenty-year old Oxford graduate, who was touring the area, making sketches of Caucasian peaks for an English publisher. Despite their enthusiasm for the expedition, neither brother was prepared to break this agreement and lose the retainer fee.

Finally, Boris Kosloff offered a possible solution. "You come," he suggested, turning to Barnes. "Draw on top."

Barnes looked at Ed and smiled. "Would you take me?" he asked enthusiastically.

Silently, Ed surveyed the six-foot-tall, athletic figure standing before him. "What climbs have you done?" he said.

"Several in the English Lake District and Scotland," Barnes said, reeling off a number of climbs, many of which were familiar to Ed, and he was not impressed.

"Have you done any snow and ice climbing?"

"Only one, in the Alps, Mont Blanc."

Ed frowned. Clearly Barnes had a little experience, but Ed doubted it was enough for what he believed lay ahead on C10. There was a long pause while Ed continued to study the man standing in front of him.

"You realize," he said at last, "your limited experience could put the whole expedition in danger."

Barnes looked down and nodded.

"I take care of him." Boris butted in. "He come or I not go. If I not go brother Lev not go."

"Show me what clothing you have," Ed said, ignoring Boris's comment.

Barnes rushed into the next room and, in a moment, returned with woolen long-johns, shirts, sweaters, breeches, cotton puttees and a belted tweed jacket slung over his left arm, while in his right hand he held a pair of heavily nailed climbing boots covered in vile smelling grease.

"Crampons?" Ed said as he carefully examined the clothing piece by piece.

From the look on the faces of the three men, it was clear they had never heard the word. "How do you climb on ice without them?" Ed asked.

"Cut steps with an ice ax," Barnes said, "How else?"

"That works," Ed admitted, "but it's slow compared with using crampons. Still, if you haven't got them, cutting steps will have to do."

"I've got an ax," Barnes said enthusiastically, then paused before adding, "By the way, what are crampons?"

Ed disregarded the question. At that moment, he was torn between the threat the inexperienced Barnes might pose to the expedition and the inevitable delay in starting out should he decide not to take him. Finally, time won out and, reluctantly, Ed agreed that Barnes could join the party. They would leave in a week.

The day dawned brightly, with only a few wispy clouds streaking the sky. They tackled the glacier in two separate groups. Ed, Mark and Ken, with their ten-point crampons attached to the soles of their climbing boots, were on one rope, while the Kosloffs and Barnes, armed only with ice axes, were on the other. The first group surged up the huge, serac-strewn face of the glacier, while the second group, forced to cut steps in the ice, moved more slowly.

Despite this, both parties made good progress and, taking advantage of the weather, were up to the steep sloping North/West Ridge by noon. To avoid the gale force winds that, even on a day like this, swept across the crest, they started to traverse this section below the ridge on the Eastern side.

Climbing steadily, they had reached 11,500 ft. by mid-afternoon. Finding a comparatively level area of snow in the lee of the ridge, they decided to halt for the day. They erected their two-man tents and prepared a meal of thick slices of mutton heated over a primitive stove, a large loaf of Russian bread and mugs of steaming tea. As the sun sank behind the ridge, the air became markedly colder and, by the time darkness descended, each man was thankful to climb into his sleeping bag.

The night passed quietly, the only sound being the howling of the wind off the ridge. At four a.m., the party was up and about, preparing to breakfast on the remains of the previous night's meal. Within the hour, they were ready for their assault on the summit.

The sight of the sun peeping over the massive dome of C10 promised the weather of the previous day would hold. Leaving their tents and supplies behind, the party roped up with Ed in the lead, followed by Hardman and Phelps, while Barnes was nursed along in the rear by the two Kosloff brothers. For two hours, they worked their way to the end of the ridge. Here, they found their route blocked by an exposed rock face rising, almost vertically, for more than two hundred feet. As Alexei had said, the glass-like surface appeared to be devoid of any handholds or footholds.

Ed was convinced the only way to negotiate this obstacle was by the use of pitons and ropes, although there were no visible cracks where the spikes could be hammered home. At the same time, he wondered if Barnes would be up to this method of climbing. The only hope was that the Oxford man's strength and athleticism would overcome his lack of experience.

Hunched down at the foot of the rock, they discussed their options. Ed was not surprised to see Barnes listening intently to what was about to happen and, at the same time, trying to hide his fear by gazing upwards.

"David, you stay here and don't move," Ed told him. "The rest of us will split up. Boris and I will go left while you three go right. Let's see if there is a better way up."

Carefully, each party inched its way along the wall, eyes constantly searching for any flaws in the rock face. As Boris and Ed advanced, a few cracks began to appear and after half an hour they came across what they were looking for. A large chimney-like fissure about three feet wide which, as far as they could see, ran all the way to the top of the rock. The sides of the fissure were rough, and by pressing their backs against one side and their knees or feet against the other, they should, Ed believed, be able to shuffle their way up. It was certainly an easier approach than using pitons on the outer face, added to which they would be sheltered from the wind.

Ed went back to gather the rest of the party and, on his return, nodded to Boris to lead the way. Settling into the crack, Boris began to inch his way up. It was painfully slow and Ed began to wonder if they might be forced to spend another night on the mountain and that, perhaps, they should use the remaining daylight moving the camp to the foot of the wall.

After what seemed like hours, a shout from above heralded Boris's success. Now, with the rope to help, the ascent went more quickly. First Hardman, then Phelps joined Boris on the ledge above. Ed decided Barnes should go next, followed by Lev and finally himself. It took the combined strength of the three on the ledge to haul Barnes up, but finally, around lunch time, all six were on the ledge facing a short, wind-swept ice slope leading to a shoulder of rock, above which could be seen a steep snow slope.

Bent almost double against the biting wind, they edged up the first slope with Boris in the lead. Barnes slipped and slithered but Lev never allowed him to be more than a step in front and, keeping the rope taut, managed to guide him to the shoulder without mishap. Now, they moved onto the south face to negotiate the shoulder. Lev took over the lead, moving carefully up the steep snow slope to avoid starting an avalanche. The summit was well in sight now. After a long and difficult stride round an awkward rock that jutted out to block their path, they found a gentle snow slope was all that separated them from their goal.

"We're there," Ed screamed and, unroping, made a dash up the slope to be first on the summit. The others also unroped and followed in his footsteps. They had conquered C10 and, as though to share in their victory, the early afternoon sun broke through the clouds and bathed them in its pure light.

It was like being on top of the world. Whichever way they looked, numerous lower peaks stretched away into the far distance. Some were snowcapped, others the gray of bare rock. No one spoke, each standing in awe of the view.

"We should say a short prayer," Ed said, "for our safe delivery on the summit of this magnificent mountain."

Silently, the six men joined hands in a circle while Ed prayed aloud. "May God Almighty be with us during our descent and may we all arrive safely back in Minskia," he said in conclusion. The group echoed his "Amen."

If they were to reach their camp before dark, Ed reckoned they could spend no more than half an hour on the summit. Far from sketching the view, Barnes seemed to welcome all the rest he could get, although he continued to pronounce himself capable of negotiating the descent. At three o'clock, Ed ordered them to start down. This time, Boris took the lead, followed by Mark Hardman, David Barnes, Lev, and Ken Phelps, with Ed holding the rear spot on the rope.

The group had no difficulty negotiating the gentle snow slope but, as they took the long and difficult stride around the jutting rock, it became clear Barnes was beginning to suffer exhaustion from his efforts at high altitude. He proved incapable of taking the necessary stride. Lev, with Mark and Ken holding the rope tightly on either side, had to straddle the distance and hold Barnes in place. The steep snow slope that followed proved no easier.

By now, the young Oxford graduate was gasping heavily and his steps were short and unsteady. Using the same technique as at the rock, the group managed to guide him round the shoulder.

At the top of the steep icy slope that led to the ledge above the crack, Ed decided they should use a second rope and carefully lower Barnes down by himself.

Finally, all six arrived safely on the ledge. Here they paused for a few minutes, hoping Barnes would recover enough to negotiate the crack without mishap. Ed considered lowering the young man in a sling using a second rope but the unevenness and sharpness of the walls made such a move extremely dangerous. At best, the rope might be caught, necessitating someone to inch down to free it and, at worst, the rope might be cut, leaving an exhausted

Barnes unprotected on the most difficult part of the climb.

Boris started down and, after several minutes, shouted that he was now on the edge of the North/West Ridge. Hardman, who had held the rope for Boris, followed. Now it was Barnes's turn.

Having checked that the Oxford man was safely tied, Lev sat with his feet braced against a projecting rock, his hands paying out the rope that ran across his back and over his left shoulder. Slowly and painfully, Barnes began the descent. Ken Phelps and Ed were a few feet away, safely belayed to a large rock pinnacle. *If*, Ed thought, *we can get him down this, we should make it back to camp without major problems.* He cursed himself for letting Boris talk him into bringing Barnes in the first place. Even then, he had had a feeling that they were courting disaster.

Time dragged as Barnes continued to inch downwards. Suddenly, there was a shout from below and the rope went slack. Quickly, Lev hauled it taut again before looking across at Ed and Ken. "Rope stuck," he said.

Carefully, Ed edged over to the top of the crack and peered down. The angle of the rope was wrong. Instead of going straight down, it ran at an angle, suggesting that Barnes, for some reason— maybe fear—had moved further into the crack rather than staying on the outer edge. Now, either Barnes had to untie the rope and continue his descent unprotected or someone from above had to climb down and free it.

Ed moved over to Lev. "Go," he said as he took over the rope.

Lev nodded as he removed the rope from around his waist and made ready to enter the crack. With no rope to protect him, the Russian slowly edged his way down, following the path of the stuck rope. One slip and he knew he would hurtle to his death on the rocks below.

Despite the cold, sweat poured down Ed's face as he held the rope taut and waited for a tug from Lev to say he had found the problem. After what seemed like hours, it came and Ed allowed the rope to go slack. With a racing heart he waited for Lev to free it from its obstruction.

Suddenly the stillness was broken by screams as if all the banshees in Ireland had been let loose, quickly followed by the thunderous rumble of falling rock. The rope tore through Ed's hands, cutting through his heavy woolen mittens and searing his palms. Then, the only sound was that of the howling wind.

Ken and Ed crept forward and, together, they peered over the rock ledge. The sight that met their eyes was horrifying. Four black shapes were hurtling down the side of the ridge, pursued by a fast moving mountain of snow, all heading for the precipice that fell away to the glacier over a thousand feet below. They watched helplessly, tears in their eyes and the roar of the avalanche in their ears, as their comrades clutched desperately at anything in a futile effort to check their slide. One by one, they disappeared over the edge followed by the snow slide.

The two men sat on the ledge, mouths dry, too petrified to move, their nerves completely shattered. How long they sat, they never knew, but darkness was descending before they plucked up courage to inch their way down the crack. By now, it was too late to make camp. They spent a sleepless night crunched into the base of the rock chimney.

In the morning light, they tried to piece together what had happened. Part of the track left by their companions was still clearly visible, emanating from the base of the crack.

With that and the screams they had heard while on the ledge above, they surmised that Barnes had either lost his nerve or been too exhausted to continue pressing his back and knees against the walls while waiting for the rope to be freed. If so, when it *was* finally free, he would have dropped a few feet before it tightened again. Lev, totally unaware of Barnes situation, would have still been holding the rope and the jerk would have been enough to drag him from his precarious position.

Whatever the reason, it appeared the two men then plunged down the chimney, knocking Boris and Mark Hardman, waiting at the base, off their feet. The melee of tangled bodies must have disturbed the treacherous snow, causing it to start sliding down the side of the ridge, taking the four men with it. Before anyone had time to recover, all four had lost control and were plunging to their deaths.

For several minutes, Ed and Ken stood quietly, staring in horror at the scene of the disaster before Ed mumbled, "I think we should say a prayer."

Both knelt at the foot of the chimney. "Lord God," Ed said quietly, "You have seen fit to take our companions into thy loving care. We pray that you gave them strength to bear their ordeal and that their suffering was short-lived. We ask that you watch over the two of us as we make our way down this mountain and deliver us safely to our destination. Amen."

"Amen," echoed Ken.

Another minute passed in silence before the two men scrambled to their feet. Deciding the instability of the snow was a greater danger than the gale force winds, they continued their descent along the crest of the ridge. Progress was slow, each being well aware of the likely consequences of a false step.

By late morning, they came upon their campsite. The three tents were exactly as they had left them. Here they hesitated, neither man wanting to disturb the site but each knowing that they needed their crampons to negotiate the glacier at the end of the ridge. Reluctantly, they crept inside their respective tents, quickly emerging with tears in their eyes and their crampons strung around their necks. Leaving the campsite as a memorial to their lost companions, Ed and Ken pushed on down the ridge.

By early afternoon they were at the top of the glacier, thankful to be off the treacherous snow and onto solid ice. With their crampons attached, they made short work of this final stage of their descent.

Weary and dejected, the two men trudged along the unpaved main street of Minskia towards their lodgings as gray, whirling storm clouds began to settle over the mountains surrounding the village. Exhausted, they failed to notice that the few inhabitants they passed ignored them, turning their heads away or crossing to the other side of the street.

There was no response when they knocked on the Alexei's door.

"Damn!" said Ed, turning to Ken. "You don't suppose they're both away, do you?"

"Don't know, but it looks like it."

"Where are we going to spend the night?"

As if in answer to the question, the door was thrown open and Sasha stood on the step, arms crossed over her ample bosom and a steely look in her dark, almost black eyes. She did not speak. Instead she blocked every move the men made to enter. After a few minutes, it became clear they were no longer welcome and would have to find alternative accommodation.

Suddenly, Sasha unfolded her arms and handed a piece of paper to Ed on which was scrawled one word: CHURCH.

Ed nodded.

Leaving Sasha standing on her doorstep, the men turned away and headed for the small, wooden Russian Orthodox Church building on the edge of the village. The sight that met their eyes as they entered stopped them in their tracks. In front of the altar were four crudely constructed biers, on which lay the shattered remains of their companions. As they stood staring at the sight, they heard the door behind them open and close. Turning, they found Alexei standing there. Slowly, he advanced towards them.

"You kill," he said, his voice breaking with emotion. "Go."

"Alexei," Ed said, stepping up to his erstwhile friend. "It was an accident."

"Accident, yes," Alexei said. Then, in a voice devoid of all emotion, he added, "I warn you but you go. See what you done." He flung his arms in the direction of the biers before adding, "Good friends, good climbers. Gone."

"But," Ed said, "We climbed..."

Before he had time to finish, Alexei stepped to one side and, arm outstretched, pointed at the church door. "Collect goods. Go," he roared.

After spending the night outside, huddled against the church walls, the two men returned to Alexei's house to find all their belongings dumped in the snow outside. No one was willing to guide them to the nearest railway station, although many were willing to sell them horses, being only too glad to see them leave. Finally, on the second day, they once again mounted those uncomfortable Tartar saddles and slowly made their way westwards.

They never climbed together again until five years later. At the sound of the whistle, they scrambled over the parapet of their trench and headed directly into the withering machine gun fire that raked the Somme Valley. Within seconds both men had started that long ascent up the stairway to Heaven.

About the author:

This is Bill Westhead's third time as a finalist in the Scribes Valley Short Fiction Contest. His previous stories 'Romeo and Sierra's Last Mission' and 'Cruel Justice' were finalists in 2005 and 2006 and published in the anthologies of those years—*They Do Exist!* and *Mind Trips Unlimited.*

Born in England, he and his family emigrated to Waycross, Georgia in 1973. With their children having fled the nest to start their own families, he and his wife continue to live in Waycross with their dog, Ben and cat, Oscar.

A member of Southeastern Writers Association and Coastal Writers Group he has published four historical novels *Once in Old Frederica Town, Confederate Gold, Clogs* and its sequel *The Mill.* His work has also been published in *Cricket, Animal Tales, Chicken Soup* series, the *O, Georgia!* anthology, *Crafts 'n Things* and several trade magazines.

Apart from novels and short stories, he also writes a monthly theatre column, *Footlights*, for area and local newspapers.

Currently he is working on his fifth book, *Not My War*, a memoir of his time as a child in England during World War II.

When not writing, he divides his time between his Bonsai collection and the Waycross Area Community Theatre.

SECOND PLACE

JOHNNY WANDERS
©2008 by Charles Kramer

A word drifted lazily through the rank nursing home air.
"Rose."

Johnny heard it in his room, sitting on the edge of his hospital bed, the metal rails glistening in the unusually warm May sun that poured through the window. Johnny looked out his window to the woods. Three, maybe four, hemlocks deep, it ran the length of the home's grounds to separate it from the failing strip mall.

He turned back to the photo album he had been perusing for the ten-thousandth time. Gray young men and women smiled, gave gangster stares, or laughed back at him. He paused at one that showed a young man in a long wool coat leaning jauntily against a Model T, one spat-clad foot resting on the running board.

Johnny smiled. "You handsome devil."

A young woman draped her arm around the man's shoulder. She sported a flapper dress, a cloche hat, and a devil-may-care grin.

"Rose," said Johnny, touching the girl. "God, how I missed you. And now you're back."

The Model T took them to Atlantic City. What a day. About midday, Johnny produced a new Kodak Brownie and paid the balloon man to take a picture of them.

"*I love the way you're full of surprises, Johnny,*" Rose said, *draping her arm around him.*

Johnny glanced at the door, its path barred by a wide orange mesh strip with a bright red stop sign in the middle to deter "wanderers." Johnny had too much experience with them to take the strip down. Yet it was a new Alzheimer's patient who told him about Rose. Mrs. Curtis was in the early stages of the disease, so Johnny felt sure her testimony was trustworthy.

"Rose Simmons?" she had said that first day when he welcomed her to St. James' Nursing Home. "Yes, she came to Ivory Arms a month or so ago. Sweet girl, she helped me so much. Sweet girl."

Rose Simmons, the girl whose heart he broke when he went away. Or did she break his heart when she went down to the city to cook for that white family? "I'd have married you, Rose," said Johnny as he caressed the silver-gray face looking up at him so adoringly.

"Help me!" came a voice outside the room. "Will somebody help me, please! Oh, help me!"

He knew without looking that it was Agnes. Soon, an aide would be at her side, shouting into her deaf ears as they always did.

"What do you need, Miss Agnes?"

"Help me. Won't you help me?"

"I'm trying, dear. What do you need?"

A thick splashing sound interrupted them. Another woman's voice—Johnny couldn't recognize it—cried, "Oh God, I messed myself." Running sounds neared, and then he saw two young women in their pink housekeeping uniforms and an aide in her blue hurry past. Johnny knew it was close because the stench wafted into his room almost immediately.

"Geez, Dolores, you didn't mess yourself, you messed the whole floor! What happened to your diaper?" Dolores did not say, but her silent answer sent them into a fit of giggles.

"Oh, honey, it's not a shoe!"

Other noises crowded out Dolores's response: squeaking wheelchairs, Cora screaming "Don't touch me!", and the incessant public address system. A wheelchair alarm started blaring which sent more feet scurrying.

Johnny sighed. If Rose knew how he lived, she would come for him. It would be like old times. He just knew it.

"I'd do anything for you, Johnny," she said as they walked hand-in-hand down the boardwalk.

"Anything?" he asked with a glint in his eye.

A large, muscular woman in a blue uniform appeared in his doorway, her broad confident smile lighting the room. "Hi, Mr. Walker!" she said. "Coming down to lunch?"

Johnny looked up and returned the gesture. "In a minute, Eleanor." She waved and moved to another room. Maybe Rose would take him out to lunch someday.

Johnny closed the photo album and placed it carefully on the dresser an arm's length from his bed. He pushed himself up, grabbed his cane—the gray metal kind with a gray plastic handle, and shuffled to the mirror. He buttoned the top button on his blue and green plaid dress shirt and tucked it into his black sweat pants. "You still got it, boy," he said with satisfaction.

His three best friends sat with him at a square table. Mabel, to the left, was a shriveled up 103-year-old who still wore her long, silver hair in a ponytail and had outlived her children. Agatha, to his right, was only eighty-two, overweight, and dour. The Deacon—that's all anyone ever called him—was a tall, lean, and elegant man with thick, plastic-rimmed glasses. He spoke little but had an air of serenity that made even Agatha relax.

Yet the Deacon was not serene today. Every few seconds he pulled a piece of paper out of his lap and held it up so that it nearly touched his nose. Then he gave a *humph* of disgust, shoved the paper back in his lap, and tapped impatiently on his empty plate. "Damned brother died," he said irritably.

Johnny wondered at this anger but said nothing. Agatha had no such scruples. "Shame on you, Deacon! You should never speak ill of the dead."

The Deacon waved off the comment. "He was an evil-tempered drunk. But he was also older than me, and as long as he lived on his own there was a chance the family might get me out. Now they'll just say, 'See? That's why you have to stay.'"

Johnny thought he ought to say something. "It's not that bad, old boy, is it?"

The Deacon turned on him. "Easy for you to say, Johnny. You got no family, no nobody, and you're ninety-two years old. Where else *would* you go? But me? I'm young,"—a pause—"sort of. Anyway, I got family, I can move around, and—"

Johnny never heard the rest. "Where else would you go?" rang in his ears. *Where else would you go?* And then he knew. He would go to Rose, the one person he still had.

Beautiful Rose, walking hand in hand with Johnny amidst the summer crowd, laughing at the ocean's spray. That night as they lay side-by-side in the sand, she said, "I love you, Johnny. I always will." Even when she left for New York, she kissed him and said, "I love you, Johnny."

***

Actually, the escape itself was easy. As one of the *trustees*—his word, not the home's—Johnny could freely walk the grounds. The next morning, he dressed in his usual button-down shirt but wore dress pants as well and his black leather shoes instead of sneakers. After breakfast he went out to sit on the smoker's porch.

"But, Johnny," said the woman at the front desk, "you don't smoke—and it's bad for you."

Johnny flashed his charmer's smile. "Honey, by the time I get cancer, I'll be twenty years dead."

Outside, he was assaulted by the gagging stench of cigarette smoke. How could they put up with this stuff? Johnny wondered. Yet this porch, essential to his plan, abutted the small woods and was relatively unguarded. As long as no staff came out to suck some carcinogens, he could slip away unnoticed.

There were only two residents, both bundled up in heavy winter coats. Johnny, in his trench coat, wondered how seventy-five degrees could feel so cold. From the front porch around the corner, he could hear the amplified voice of a volunteer nun leading Rosary Hour. "Hail Mary, full of grace, the Lord is with thee..." He looked down at the two smokers. As expected, both had fallen asleep, their cigarettes dangling from their fingers.

Now was his chance. Fifty paces, and he was at the first tree. Up to this point, he had broken no rules. One more step, however, meant crossing the Rubicon. One deep breath, one quick glance to make sure he was unobserved, then he slipped into the little wood, his black coat blending in with the trees.

Just like that night he helped Rose escape from her overbearing brother, running through the woods till they reached his Model T. Then a hundred-seventy odd miles to Atlantic City, laughing and holding hands the whole way. "I love you, Johnny," she said from the passenger seat. He remembered so well.

Fifty more paces and he was on the other side, walking as a free man in the parking lot of Cross Hart Plaza. He looked around and felt utterly lost.

***

The asphalt of Cross Hart Plaza was old and cracked. Gaping fissures made walking awkward at best, and implausible in the most derelict corners. The paper-lined windows formed an endless row of brown teeth, with one gap in the middle. That was *Barber Joe's,* a black void marked by a single bulb burning in the back like a uvula.

The *Ice Cream Barn,* Cross Hart's only thriving business, rose above it all. White with a fake red barn roof stuck on top, its doors opened wide in a promise of safe haven, comfort, and the familiar. Two cows standing guard in front seemed to say, "Forget everything you see around you. It isn't real. Only come inside and be at home."

Johnny turned his face toward the barn. All he could see was its white and red, which is why he failed to see the chasm before him. The toe of his tight leather shoe caught the tip of the upraised asphalt just enough to send him flying forward. Instinctively, he threw out his hands, which saved his face. Johnny's knees and hands took the brunt of the fall, and when he sat down to inspect himself, he swore.

"Damn it!" he said louder than he had said in many years. Since entering St. James', Johnny had been careful with his language. The Alzheimer's group used foul language. The nasty old men and mean old ladies nobody liked swore a blue streak. Johnny was nothing like them. But as he picked tiny rocks out of the palms of his hands, he had to admit, swearing felt good. "Shit!" he said more brazenly for the sheer joy of it. Then he laughed. Many St. James' residents fell, but few could sit up afterwards, let alone swear and laugh about it. "Oh, Johnny," he said to himself even as he sucked his breath through a pang of pain. "You're just a cut above the rest."

That's what Rose had said back in the day. "Johnny, you're just a cut above the rest." That was when she laid her head on his shoulder as she sat next to him in that blessed Model T. They rode in the dark along the dusty roads back up from Atlantic City, one of the headlights blown and the other complaining. Johnny kept driving while he whistled a jaunty tune. Rose asked him if he was worried about getting lost in all the dark, and in response, Johnny turned off the functioning headlight and drove on. Rose laughed and snuggled up closer. "Oh Johnny," she said, "You're just a cut above the rest."

Amazingly, nobody came to his aid. Or perhaps not so amazingly. There was hardly a car in the parking lot. It was still a little early for sweets, so even *Ice Cream Barn* stood in silent expectation. Johnny's eyes fell on the thing he needed now, a sidewalk. More careful of his step, he made his way to the little concrete path that connected the vacant stores. Secure once more, he tap-tap-tapped his cane against the concrete, inching forward in baby steps. Compared to St. James' halls, the distance to the barn seemed so vast.

Two stores to go and it hit him: Johnny had no money. He had no need of it at the home. Yes, they received small allowances to buy trinkets here and there, but what did he have to buy? For whom? Money was meaningless these days, as foreign a concept as all those suicide bombers he kept hearing about on the television. Yet back in the day, when Rose hung on his arm, and he knocked down milk cans with a baseball to win her a stuffed bear, he loved to flaunt his ill-gotten wealth.

Johnny became a man during the wild days of prohibition. He played his beloved fiddle at speakeasies four nights a week. His favorite had always been the roof garden joint on the building across from the Catholic Church. Johnny thought it odd the Catholic priest never complained until he saw Fr. O'Hanlen at a table on the roof garden, sharing a drink with a local moonshiner. What he loved most about that speakeasy was that he met Rose there.

She danced in the show. When it ended, she hung a little tray full of cigarettes around her neck and went from table to table selling them. "How much for the whole bunch of 'em?" he asked her with a devilish smile.

"What?" she asked.

"All of them," he said, pulling out a wad.

She beamed. "Wow, then I'll have the rest of the night off!"

"Want to go to Atlantic City?" he'd asked just like that.

She laughed.

In those illicit days, money meant something. Now it meant something again—disaster. Without it he could eat nothing, call no one, and, worse still, go nowhere. How would he catch a cab to Rose?

Johnny found a battered metal bench against the faded sign of *Mary's Beauty School*, which must have closed ten years ago. He rested his cane on his knees and slowly, elegantly rested his head in both hands. "I'm turning into one of the wanderers," he said out loud. "Forgot all about money." The words cut him like a knife to the heart, until he looked up, staring at yet another fear. "A wanderer," he said. "I just wandered away from the home. They'll take away my freedom now. They'll lock me in a chair and hook me up to one of those alarms. They'll ask me where I'm going every time I get near the elevator."

He had to come up with a plan. Johnny needed to either figure out how to get to Rose or how to break back into St. James' unnoticed. Or at least make up a really good excuse for leaving the home. What he needed now was time to think.

Johnny stared at the greenback several moments before it finally registered. Money. It sparked new life, new hope in him. He knew a dollar wouldn't even get him inside a cab, but it ought to be enough for a cone at the *Ice Cream Barn*, and that was something. He gently worked it from its lodged position, clutching his cane securely to keep his balance, then pocketed the bill and resumed his stroll to the barn.

An electronic *beep-bop* sounded as Johnny crossed the threshold. The barn was freezing. Johnny pulled his trench coat up around his neck and shivered. How long had it been since he'd stepped inside a place like this? Last outing he'd made with the home there had been a stop at an ice cream parlor, but everyone ate outside in the ninety-degree weather. It must be sixty here.

A man sat at a plastic table against the left wall eating a mountain of soft serve topped with some tan goo and colorful bits of what Johnny could only assume was candy. On the right side, a young woman wrestled with a fat preschool boy. "Just eat your ice cream, Joey," she said. "I don't want to hear no more about the playground."

Johnny shook his head but then shrugged. What did he care? He had his dollar and right there on the wall it said *Small Cone - $1.00*. He bellied up to the bar and placed his order. His smile beamed until the old white woman behind the counter said, "That'll be a dollar eight."

The "eight" hit him with a shock down the spine like that time with Rose when he accidentally grabbed the wrong part of a barbed wire fence.

She was laughing at their escape from Marcus, her brother. He made her come home every night after work, and he wouldn't let her out again until morning. Johnny sneaked through the woods and hauled her out a window with a ladder. Then they ran for it, but as he lifted one wire of a barbed wire fence, he managed to grab a barb. He yelped, Rose giggled, and somehow it was all right.

Johnny was quick to recover. "It says a dollar."

"Plus tax."

"Don't you have a senior discount?"

"For ice cream?"

"Listen, honey," he started, "I'm ninety-two years old—"

Johnny knew he had her. He saw it in her eyes. Probably retired from the phone company but with insufficient pension to make it, and insufficient imagination to come up with a more interesting retirement job.

He was just gearing up for the one-sided battle of wits, when a dime chinked onto the counter. "Get the man his ice cream, okay?" Johnny turned wide-eyed to see the man of the mountainous sundae standing next to him. "I think I can afford eight cents," the man said with a tired smile. A moment's hesitation in which the man gave Johnny a quick once-over, then the man said, "I'm Paul. Want to join me?" He motioned to the table, now covered with paper napkins. The ice cream looked more like Mount St. Helen's with half its top blown off.

Johnny shrugged and shuffled to the table. Paul sat facing the door, one eye periodically darting to it as if checking for a new arrival. Johnny was glad to have his back to the door, that way none of the nursing home staff would see him if they walked by on their way to the bus stop.

"So, what's a nice guy like you doing with only one dollar?" asked Paul casually.

Johnny sensed an interrogation coming on. He knew about interrogations and wanted no part of it. "Thanks for the dime, my friend," he said with his most charming smile. "I won't forget my wallet next time." He rose to leave.

Paul stood as well. "Sorry," he said. "Stupid question. Just trying to make conversation. Haven't seen you here before, and I'm here a lot," he added, patting his belly. Paul had to be middle-aged, with thinning dark hair and a pair of wire-rimmed glasses. His suit was clean but had seen plenty of action.

Johnny pegged him for a detective right away, which presented both a problem and an opportunity. Johnny sat back down, his smile more relaxed though he was thinking fast. "Apology accepted, Officer," he finally said.

Now it was Paul's turn to gape. "How did you—?"

"Your gun," Johnny pointed to the shoulder holster. "Either you're a detective or a gangster, and gangsters don't kick in tax for little old men."

"I can see you're a sharp guy," said Paul, unconsciously checking his holster. "Are you really ninety-two?"

"Every day of it," said Johnny proudly. "The secret to long life is to never smoke or get married." Paul raised his eyebrows. "On the other hand," Johnny added, noting Paul's wedding ring, "long life isn't everything, is it? Take me for example. Ninety-two and never married. Lost a girl once. Worst mistake of my life."

"What happened to her?"

Johnny had baited the hook. Now to reel Paul in. "Funny thing. She moved away, long time ago. But now she's back. We were going to meet here."

"Why here?" asked Paul.

Johnny shrugged. "It's where she wanted. Who am I to argue?"

"How'd you get here, anyway?" asked Paul.

Johnny was ready. "A friend dropped me off on his way out of town. I was supposed to get a ride home with Rose."

"Rose?"

"The woman. My old, uh, girlfriend." Johnny's eyes became moist but he forged ahead. "Only now I'm beginning to wonder if she's coming." Johnny looked at his pocket watch. "I was late, so maybe she didn't wait for me." They stared at each other uncomfortably for a minute.

Paul took one last bite of his remaining ice cream hill, then stuffed the napkins into the plastic bowl. "Do you think you should call her?" he asked.

Johnny shook his head. "Don't have the number with me and I can't remember it. Keep it written down in my wallet of course, but it's at home." He looked at Paul with a sheepish grin. "You, uh, don't think you could do me a favor, do you?"

Paul gave the smile of a man who knew. "Sure. Where do you live?"

***

Ivory Arms dominated Market Street between North Division and Assumption. Ten stories of white brick and glass. The roof boasted a chain-link fence, a stupendously large air conditioning unit, and a small rooftop garden. A canopy welcomed guests and residents. Across the street spread a playground filled with young men. Johnny recognized the type, and he knew they were up to no good. After all these years, punks were still the same. "You cops ought to do something about these guys."

Paul snorted, but as they pulled up to Ivory Arms, he kept a wary eye on the park.

Johnny climbed shakily out of the car. With a groan and a stretch, he looked up at the imposing building and shivered. What to do? What if Rose didn't remember him? What if she hated him for never coming after her? Hadn't he promised? Back then. He turned to Paul and waved his thanks.

Paul nodded but did not move. "I'll just wait till you get inside," he called through the open window.

Johnny started for the Ivory Arms, still trembling, a frightened little boy. The door felt cold and hard in his hand. No automatic door openers here. He entered a foyer with a bewildering array of buttons, each with a name attached. Arndt, Attwater, Beyer. He skipped down the line. Rayburn, Rothenburg, Rugen, Satterly,

Sandberg, Scott, Sharp, Simon, Skidmore, Slaughter, Slick... He ran his hands up and down the list again. Scott, Sharp, Simon, Skidmore. Where was Simmons? Where was Rose?

A buzzing noise startled him. The door that divided the foyer from the hallway was buzzing. He pulled the handle. Again, hard and cold, and heavy. Tottering uncertainly into the large hall, he encountered a tall reception desk. A woman who could have been the *Ice Cream Barn* lady's twin smiled warmly at him. "May I help you? You looked a little confused out there."

Confused? Like a wanderer? God, no, thought Johnny. He tucked his fear behind his disarming smile. "Yes, thank you," he said. "I was told an old friend of mine was living here, but I can't find her name."

"What's her name? I can double check for you." He told her. She looked through her own list on the desk and gave a small frown, flipping one sheet of paper after another, then back again. "No, no Rose Simmons. Are you sure you don't mean Rose Simon? She moved in a couple of months ago. About yea tall," she indicated the top of her head. "She said she was seventy-six but looks like she could be in her fifties."

Johnny's heart sank. Seventy-six? No, no, no. "No Rose Simmons about yea tall?" he asked, hand at his chin, maybe ninety years old?"

The woman laughed. "I'm sorry, sir, this is a seniors apartment, not a nursing home. I don't think we have anybody here that old. Most find they need assisted living at that age."

Johnny sniffed. "Hmmm. Well, thank you." He turned and made for the door, a new kind of shaking working its way through his body: anger at the slight, blended with confusion and embarrassment...and fear.

Just like the day about a week after Atlantic City. They sat by the Hudson River together, watching a train speed south toward Manhattan. In one hand he held a freshly developed photograph of the two of them leaning jauntily against the Model T. Rose squeezed his hand and said, "Johnny?"

"Hmmm?"

"I'm leaving."

"I'll take you home."

"No, Johnny. I'm moving to New York. Marcus don't want me to dance no more. I'm working for a rich white family down there. It's good money."

He stared at her.

A Nash 697 pulled up, and Marcus, big and dumb, leaned out. "Let's go, girl!" he yelled.

She looked at him with a weak smile. "You're a cut above the rest, Johnny." She kissed him on the cheek and turned.

"I'll come for you, Rose," said Johnny. "Some day."

Johnny sat down on a bench that leaned against the building and stared off into space. Had he been paying attention, he would have seen Paul. But he didn't. He *felt* him.

Paul plunked his considerable frame down on the bench next to Johnny. "No luck, huh?"

"What?" Johnny gaped at the officer in horror. "I thought you left."

Paul unwrapped a lollipop and offered it to Johnny who shook his head. Paul shrugged and popped it in his own mouth. "Yeah, well I thought you might want a ride home."

Johnny jerked his head around so hard it hurt. "This is—"

"—not your home," interrupted Paul. He reached over to Johnny's left wrist and pulled on the nursing home bracelet. "As smart as you are, Johnny, I thought you'd hide this better. Senior residences don't have these. Nursing homes do."

Their eyes met.

"So," said Paul. "It *was* a woman, wasn't it?"

***

Johnny's head hung as they entered St. James'. His cane tapped erratically on the linoleum floor as he barely mustered the energy to lift it.

Velma at the front desk screamed when she saw him. "Mr.

Walker!" she squealed. "Where have you been?"

Johnny noticed, as if in slow motion, that Velma's long dark bangs danced along her forehead when she got excited. Out of habit, he hitched up his charmer's smile, and struggled to think of a good answer.

"I am terribly sorry," said Paul. "I think I forgot to sign the right book when I took Uncle Johnny out. He was thinking about it the whole time and finally insisted that we return."

"Uncle?" asked Velma incredulously.

"Great uncle," said Paul.

"You're white," said Velma.

"By marriage," said Paul without batting an eye.

Johnny beamed. He liked this guy.

Velma turned to him suspiciously. "Johnny?"

"You should see his mother," Paul laughed.

Johnny giggled.

Velma glowered at them like a school principal. "You know everyone's been going crazy looking for you. We were about to call the police. There's going to be a lot of papers to fill out, too."

Paul pulled out his badge. "I can handle paperwork. So, Johnny," he said redirecting his gaze. "Want to go out again next Saturday? Renegades home opener."

Johnny stared, gaping. "Yeah?"

"It'll be fun," he said. "You don't mind if I bring the kids?"

"You'd better sign him out properly next time!" said Velma.

Johnny returned to his room an hour later. He missed lunch during his adventure and would have to wait for dinner. Rose was gone, and he figured he would never see her again.

But Johnny had made a friend, he was home, and he wasn't a wanderer.

He was alive.

About the author:

Charles Kramer is known to most folks as Chuck. He is an Episcopal priest and serves as rector at St. James' Church in Hyde Park, New York, the one-time spiritual home of Franklin and Eleanor Roosevelt.

Like most people who claim to be writers, he has been writing all his life. He wrote for the school paper in high school, used his study hall to come up with morbid stories with his friend Scott and dreamed about growing up to become Erma Bombeck.

His Freshman year in college was spent at Ripon College where he wrote for the school paper and had his own humor column called "A Sort of Genius." James Thurber fans will recognize that as the title of a Thurber short story. When he transferred to Indiana University in his junior year, Charles majored in Journalism and German literature.

After earning his Masters in German, he went to seminary to become a priest. That's what he's been doing ever since. He's served in Peekskill, NY; Morganton, NC; and now in Hyde Park where he's lived with my family for the past ten years. For five of those years he wrote another column called "Town and Church" for the local paper. He gave it up to write a novel (as yet unpublished), but still writes a blog called "Web and Church" (www.webandchurch.blogspot.com).

Writing short stories are his form of relaxation. Often, he writes them for—and with—his children. Some serve as springboards for sermons or columns. Charles enjoys playing tuba and recorder and also has fun coaching youth soccer and attempting to play ice hockey.

THIRD PLACE

THE FIRST GENERAL ORDER
©2008 by Joni Bour

The uniform and the soldier were inseparable and had shared many things. Both the living through and survival of that year shaped everything the man did—or didn't do—ever since. Just one year made a young man old before he had finished being young.

The soldier and his uniform had been together through Boot Camp when one whispered the Three General Orders to the other and won the admiration of their peers. When one crawled through the mud, the other got dirty and when one ran five miles, it was certain the other was equally soaked with sweat. They graduated as a Private First Class and stood at attention alongside the young man's father as his mother snapped a picture. When the soldier's father had grasped his shoulder and reminded him to keep his head down and his butt in a foxhole, years later the uniform was still imprinted with the memory of the father's wisdom. The soldier had tried unsuccessfully to comfort his mother with one final hug as he boarded a plane for Vietnam and, though he knew he failed to relieve her fears, the hint of her perfume and feel of her salty tears brought him comfort as he sat in a plane full of other American sons with tear-stained lapels.

The two thought they were ready and trained for war, but their hard lesson learned was that no one has ever been prepared for the evil man heaps upon another. They slept in holes half filled with mud and stood watch as the hardening soldier ate peaches from a can and wiped his mouth on his sleeves. They sweated pounds of salt and fought elephant grass, bugs, and the decay of their morale. The uniform took everything life and death dealt the soldier: blood, sweat, filth and even chemicals dropped from above by his very own country. The uniform was more than just fatigues; it was the soldier's identity, shield, and friend.

The soldier had precious few friends in the time of war. In fact, he was afraid to care about much more than what he wore on his back and carried in his own two hands. So the warrior made a decision to care only for his girl back home and his buddy who had been with him through it all. Until one day, the even harder soldier was betrayed by the girl who wrote in her letter that she could no longer love a man who volunteered to die in a far-off war she could not support. This was more proof to the man that he needed only what he wore on his back and carried in his hands.

This was driven all the way home when, only days later, his buddy was taken away as well, killed when he stepped on a landmine. The soldier had quickly wiped his tears and snotty nose on his sleeve and roughly protested when the Sergeant told him that he would be escorting his buddy's remains home.

Truth be told, the soldier was afraid to go home, for he had been so long in-country and away from the real world, that emotion, politeness, and even hot running water were distant memories. Still, the Sergeant had insisted, so the soldier squared up his shoulders and did the unthinkable: prepared to go home. He cleaned up, shaved, and put on his dress uniform with the lanyard attached to his shoulder that indicated his specially appointed detail and did the right thing: he took a hero home.

On the long plane ride home, he sat stoic, not saying a single word, and communicated with only a nod once in a while. Mostly, he stared down at the buttons on his uniform and tried to make sense of his conflicts. He felt relief at having lived, and guilt that his buddy had not, and found no common ground between the two. He left the plane in Seattle to face a small crowd of shouting people when a girl walked right up in his face and spit on his chest. He had been trained to kill a man without question and he could have then, but his training failed as he stood there all alone in a crowd, dumbfounded, insulted and betrayed by his very own country.

He did not want to attend the burial of his only buddy and would have preferred to climb into a bottle, or at least a plane back to 'Nam, but again, he squared his shoulders and did the right thing. When the funeral was done, he headed straight back to the jungle where, indeed, he was safer.

He returned to Vietnam to finish his tour because that was what he had been trained to do. When his tour was over, he was afraid of going home, afraid he would not fit in, afraid he was abandoning men who needed him. But, eventually, he pulled himself together and in the cleanest uniform he owned, went home. Again, when he arrived at the airport back in the "real world" there were signs that said, "End the war" and "Stop killing the babies"; and though he had no part in starting that awful war and had certainly killed no babies, he began feeling the hint of shame, hung his head down and walked quickly into a world that did not welcome him home.

His mother had nearly fainted when she saw him walk through the door of his childhood home, shocked he had forgotten to write her to say he was coming home. She fell to her knees in thankful prayer as he walked through the house, up the stairs, into the attic, and tossed his duffle bag and all the evidence of his year in Vietnam to the furthest corner of the dimly lit space. He had started to walk away, but returned, placing a large box of old clothes and a pile of magazines on top of the beat up and smelly bag.

When he had first come home, it had taken probably four months before he could sleep in a bed instead of on the cold, hard floor and for a month or so he had eaten like a man being offered his last meal, shoveling, dunking, and reaching across others without the slightest comment or apology. More than once he forgot to take a shower for a week or so at a time, but when he remembered, he would stand under the hot running water until it ran icy cold.

For a while he used language that was unsuitable in nearly any company or would choose not to speak at all for hours and even days. Many months later, still living in his parents' home, he noticed while looking for a winter coat in the back of his closet that his uniforms had been hung neatly next to his high school letterman jacket, and he smiled, knowing his mother was the one who had sneaked them there.

For the first few years, the soldier's mother pestered him to talk about the war and to "move on." She eventually stopped pestering him about going to the VFW Hall and just begged him to live. When eventually he became ill and was told he had a cancer associated with Agent Orange, she sought solace in the darkest corner of his closet and cried only a mother's tears upon the same lapel her tears had dampened some thirty-seven years before. Perhaps she found comfort in the uniform because it had stood sentry all these years, maybe it reminded her of her son as he once was, or maybe it represented those who had murdered her son with their evil war. The fact that he had been the walking wounded for thirty years didn't change the fact that "THEY" had killed her only son. The fact that his body was still alive did not change the belief in her heart that part of him was dead. His own country had taken his spirit while the chemical companies took his body, one piece at a time.

He had struggled and found work as a carpenter, been married twice, a father once, and had a friend in almost no one. Eventually he had moved from his parents' home, preferring to live alone and wasn't much for socializing. He had packed everything when he moved, except the uniforms, but somehow, undoubtedly by his mother's hand, his uniforms had found their way again into the solitary corner of his closet. He avoided crowds and events with loud noises for fear he would embarrass himself, like the time he was at his own father's military funeral and when the shots were fired in respect, he had "hit the dirt" before he even realized where he was and his mother cried more tears. He was pretty sure there was something wrong, but it never occurred to him that he might get help.

Tired of his self-imposed isolation, the man did the only thing he could think of. He went to the darkest reaches of his closet where his mother had often retreated and pulled down the only things in his life that had refused to run away, never let him down, and never once left their post. He realized with no small amount of sappy poetry that they had fulfilled the First General Order better than any man; for they had guarded everything within their post and had never given up, until now, when being relieved. To his surprise, for the first time in a very long while, his tears flowed freely and, as it had always been, they fell upon the lapel that had grown salty with sorrows of his war.

After a moment, carrying the fragments of his year in Vietnam, he walked out, closing the door on the life he no longer needed. He drove to a local park where he had seen a traveling Vietnam Veterans Memorial on display that week. He pulled into the parking lot and three times failed to get both feet out of the truck. He prayed in a way he had never done before and finally lifted himself up and out of the beaten-up truck. He pulled on the uniform jacket and, though it didn't fit as well as it had, he immediately stood tall and strong like the soldier and man he had once been proud to be and walked slowly towards the black and white monument to wasted lives.

He felt himself drowning in the sea of names of buddies, comrades, fathers and sons and could not find his way. Realizing he hadn't even known what he was searching for and without knowing why, he stopped, removed his cap and began to weep. His body shook and his knees grew weak as he broke down in tears and leaned against the silent witness to his thirty-seven years of hate, shame, and unbearable loneliness.

With no more tears to shed, he shoved his hands deep into the pockets of his jacket and his left hand grasped the cool steel band that represented another forgotten and betrayed American son. He had worn the band as a debt of honor for many years until one day when, noting its engraved lettering had been worn nearly smooth, he finally accepted the fact that the world did not care. Unable to wear it, unable to toss it away, he had removed the bracelet from his own scarred wrist and had placed it in this same pocket.

There were many people who passed by the kneeling man that day, though none seemed to notice his distress. He leaned forward and pressed his forehead against the cold, unyielding truth of the memorial and felt the embrace of countless heavenly comrades. He stayed there awhile, just leaning into their arms, the way a child would find comfort in his mother's arms, until, as if reacting to an order, he stood straight up, slowly removed his uniform jacket and folded it with the same precise movement as he had once folded the flag over his buddy's casket. He leaned forward and whispered words no one else heard, kissed its salty lapel, then ran his fingers gently over the nearly smooth engraved letters that read ***TSGT Bennie L Dexter 09 May 1966*** on the aging POW bracelet and returned it to the protective pocket of the uniform. With one final motion, he snapped a slow respectful salute, turned on his heel and once again disappeared, unrecognized and anonymous to the world.

About the author:

Joni Bour is a native Oregonian and works in elementary school special education. Describing herself, she says, she is a searcher, believer, and rebel. She says above all things she is a believer in what others might consider lost causes and knows that tenacity is faith. Every day she sees things that other people would not have thought possible, that happened because someone believed it could should and would. Joni has held a fascination with the veterans of the Vietnam War all of her life. She says she has no idea why, but even as a child growing up in the 60's and 70's she would take every opportunity to study them, not so much the war, but the men and women who served there, who they were, why they were, and what they had become after the war. She spends much of her free time working on veteran related projects, such as working at traveling memorials, volunteering for the Veterans History Project for the Library of Congress, writing book reviews for books written about the Vietnam War and has been sought out by veteran authors to write forewords and afterwords for their books.

MOHAWK MAN
©2008 by F. Kavanagh

Walter D. Lee Reynolds, one of my favorite students, is also one of my favorite characters: self-proclaimed redneck with a red Mohawk about four inches wide and an inch high. Two weeks before the end of his senior year, he dyed it a heavy black—just the Mohawk part, not the sidewalls.

On the next-to-last day of school, he came to my room to say his car wouldn't start: dead battery.

"Do you want to use my car for a jump?" I offered.

"Naw, woud'n do enny good. 'Really just wanna go'da Wal-Mart 'n git a new battery."

Knowing Wal-Mart was only about a mile from school but also that he once walked the fifteen miles to New Braunfels, I told him he could use my ancient, gray-flecked Honda.

"Ya mean it?" he exclaimed, freckles practically jumping off his beaming face.

"Sure, but let me give you this, just in case one of those big bad wolves stops you on the road." I wrote a note acknowledging my permission for him to use my car, with various identifying numbers. He returned a half hour later, a curious air surrounding him. He resembled a husky orange tabby that'd just swallowed a canary.

"Did you get it?"

"Yeah. Thanks fer lettin' me use yer car." He hem-hawed and tugged at a slightly torn pocket of his jeans. "I got ya a little present. It's liquid—that's th' only clue I'll give you. You'll figger it out."

"You didn't leave a beer in my car, did you?"

"Naw, it's nuthin' like that."

I figured it's a liter of Dr. Pepper, or maybe some bottled water, my preference. A few hours later I went to my car for the twenty-minute drive home. I saw no drink, illicit or otherwise, anywhere on, in, or under gashes in the upholstery. I ignored the urge to bang the end of the trunk (the only way to pop it open). The trusty engine started instantly, as usual, and then I indeed "figgered it out." My tank was full.

Two evenings later at graduation—a teacher's ultimate day of gratification—I entered the most sacred of public buildings in the state of Texas: a Class 5A football stadium. I sat down on the field in the first row of faculty chairs that faced graduates from the sideline. I would be able to see up close their faces as they returned to their seats, diplomas in grasp at last, as their gold gowns would flap in the hot breeze. Awaiting the opening events, I scanned for various faces and found a few smiling at me, waving a thumbs up, just nodding happily, or hollering "Mr. K!" Then I heard the distinctive twanged voice of my favorite red redneck shouting his fond name for me:

"Kavan-haw!"

I spied him, center row halfway back, forty feet away. An ear-to-ear grin overpowered his sidewalls and mortar board, the latter pushed precariously up by his black 'Hawk.

"Thanks for the liquid," I called to him. He nodded, grinning even more.

When he later thumped down the ramp with his diploma, the usual whooping prevailed from the stands as well as from him. He then turned, hands and arms waving and pointing toward me, like a runway brakeman directing a pilot, as he began to bellow:

"THIS IS THE MAN! THIS! IS! THE! MAN!"

I stood and gave him a bear hug. We exchanged thanks and the usual masculine slams on the back.

After he returned to his seat, a revelation hit me. His proclamation was not the usual "Yoo da' man." No, Walter D. Lee Reynolds, master of slang like *Ya'mama*, and *Crackhead*, and *Aw, les jus' go'da Hooters*, a redheaded South Texan who took it upon himself to tutor the exchange student from Uzbekistan in Americanisms before and during speech class, chose to praise his speech and English teacher in completely perfect public usage—and in complete sentences.

About the author:

Frank Kavanagh has taught English and/or speech in central Texas for 23 years, including the past seven at Seguin HS. He began his writing career as a part-time sportswriter at the Port Arthur News one week after high school graduation, but a grade of 13 (yes, out of a 100) on his first college calculus test meant he would not continue the family engineering tradition. He has degrees from Lamar University and the University of Texas; a wife, a teenage son, and two twenty-something daughters.

THE MOST GLORIOUS DAY
©2008 by Vickie Clasby

All was calm and white on the snowy morning after Christmas. Dozens of birds flocked around the tree outside the window, picking pieces of popcorn from the garland Brad had fashioned from freshly popped corn and a needle and thread, just the way he had always done with his mother each Christmas. The snow covering the ground looked more beautiful and shimmering than could be possible in reality, more like what one would experience in a dream. Whiter, glitterier, more exquisite.

Despite the bright beauty of the morning, Brad's mood was dark. He was stationed by the window, surveying the winter scene while reading the heavy local paper which was filled with colorful fliers advertising door-buster savings for intrepid post-holiday shoppers. He wanted no part of the festivities. Not after the wasted time he'd spent shopping for the perfect gift for his bride. If only her response to the gift had been compensatory. He hated shopping and, truth be told, had only forced himself the week before Christmas to begin thinking about a proper gift. But once he set himself to the task, he approached it as all tasks: analytically and with conviction. He surveyed Ellie's wardrobe, habits, preferences, and carefully considered their budget. He decided that Ellie needed a new watch. She certainly could not continue wearing that unsightly sport watch with the black plastic band. He felt she needed something more grown-up, more elegant, but not ostentatious or terribly expensive. Based on her other jewelry

51

items, he surmised that she would prefer a watch of stainless steel or silver instead of gold. He determined the amount he could comfortably spend and set out one evening after work to compare brands, styles and prices. After narrowing the choices down to five acceptable offerings, he selected the least expensive and allowed the clerk to wrap the gift. He was quite pleased with his purchase, and proudly placed it under the tree when he got home.

On Christmas morning, he insisted she open her gift first. He anxiously awaited the moment when she opened the box. How disappointed he was when she failed to express the sort of elation he had expected! How could she not be pleased? She quickly closed the box and gathered a package from under the tree for him to open. Instinctively his face reddened, and he felt a sense of rejection for the watch and for himself. He steeled himself, determined not to show his feelings, and took the carefully wrapped gift from Ellie. He knew she had wrapped it herself, because he had seen evidence of the wrapping paraphernalia in the dining room. He hoped she hadn't spent too much, but also hoped she'd spent a comparable sum to what he'd spent.

He pulled the wrapping away from the flat rectangular box and opened the lid to reveal a rather large binder. A photo album with the word *MEMORIES* embossed on the cover. He looked at Ellie and noticed the expectant look on her face. When he opened the book, he saw pictures from his childhood; baby pictures, his first birthday, pictures of his mother and father proudly holding him. He saw his life lovingly chronicled through pictures that he had stored in a box in the top of their closet. Certainly a sweet gift, but not what he had hoped for. He had needed a new watch also, and a new topcoat; maybe a pair of leather gloves or a new wallet. He tried to hide his disappointment and thanked her. She embraced him and kissed him gently, but he knew she felt his lack of enthusiasm for the gift she had spent many hours preparing for him.

They spent the rest of the day together, preparing and enjoying the Christmas meal, listening to music, playing in the snow, but the disappointment was ever present, just beneath the surface like a dull headache.

He knew in his heart that he was often cold, unlike Ellie who cared for every stray cat, wounded bird, depressed colleague and perfect stranger in the grocery line. The grocery line was, in fact, where they had met. She was in line ahead of him, with three very large bags of dog food in her cart. She saw him eyeing the dog food and explained that she was taking a donation to the animal shelter. They chatted about dogs, and she explained that so many people abandon their pets, and he remembered thinking that he had never once in his life had a conversation with anyone in the grocery.

After she paid for her purchase, he very uncharacteristically offered to help load the bags in her car. Ten months later they were married. How very different they were. How on Earth had they been paired together? God certainly had a sense of humor, even if Brad did not.

In the year Brad and Ellie had been together, the life he had known had been all but obliterated. Their courtship had been swift, and he felt he barely knew her. But she had been so smitten with him, he assumed they were meant to be together or she, like countless other women, would have utterly ignored him. He couldn't fathom what she had seen in him. He was not warm or friendly or handsome or charming. The only thing he had going for him was his intellect, and that was the thing which impressed her least. She often told him that he analyzed things too much, and encouraged him to just breathe in life. He just didn't know how.

Soon after they met, his mother died very suddenly. He flew home for the funeral, and came back with a box of pictures. That was all that remained of his family. His father died when Brad was a baby, and there were no siblings. He'd stowed the box in the closet and never opened it, choosing to go on with life as though nothing had happened. He never spoke to Ellie about his family, choosing to explain that he lived in the present, not in the past.

Brad stared out the window, watching the birds eat the

popcorn, and thought of his mother. Every year when he visited, she made him sit with her and string the popcorn. He never understood why it was such an important ritual, but he'd never objected. They would sit quietly, threading the popcorn onto the string with the needle, sometimes not even speaking, then take the popcorn garland outside and wind it around the blue spruce which grew larger each year.

This year, the first after her death, he felt strangely compelled to carry on the tradition, and he and Ellie had wrapped the garland around the small pine tree outside the window. Ellie thought it was a wonderful idea, and commented on how much fun it would be to watch the birds enjoy their Christmas present. She seemed to enjoy it more than he did, even though it was his tradition. She even took a photograph of him standing next to the tree after it was adorned with the popcorn garland. Knowing Ellie, she would want to take another picture each year, and then have their future children join in when they were old enough. She would collect the pictures year by year, and comment on how much bigger the tree was, and how the children had changed.

Her sentimentality was sometimes annoying to him, and he wondered if, over time, it would annoy him less or perhaps more. Ellie was a good person, kind and loving, and he often felt she deserved more and probably needed more love than he had to give. Maybe he shouldn't have married her so quickly. Not that he would spend his life with her in misery, but would she be happy with him? Would she even know she was unhappy, or was she willing to live with only a fraction of the happiness she could have known had she met someone more like herself? He felt confused by these thoughts which were, arguably, the deepest personal thoughts he'd experienced. He was analytical about information, but not about feelings.

He was surprised at the very fact that he was considering the future of his relationship with the person who cared most for him. He knew he loved Ellie, but he'd never before considered the vast emotional differences between them. He'd been so amazed that she cared for him at all that he'd plunged headlong into the relationship. Of course, he analyzed the facts. Ellie was attractive, well educated, soft spoken, mannerly, and attentive. These were all traits that were acceptable to Brad, and he enjoyed her company. She also was very respectful of his privacy and his need to be alone with his thoughts, never demanding too much of his time or attention.

For someone like Brad, this was the true litmus test. But as he thought about the last several months with Ellie, he realized she had been gently, subtly transforming him. She encouraged his solitary pursuits, but also invited him to accompany her in her pursuits. With Ellie, he'd started attending weekly worship services. He'd spent Saturday mornings sorting and tagging discarded clothing at the local charity thrift store. He'd started to notice more of the world around him, and realized that his life was very blessed and secure. Before Ellie, he'd never noticed or cared about the inequities or unfairness around him. Although he couldn't call himself an altruist, he had definitely started to recognize opportunities for change in the world.

Brad glanced over at the Christmas tree, and noticed the memory book that Ellie had made for him. He hadn't touched it since he opened the package yesterday. His face burned with shame for the lack of gratitude he had expressed. He picked up the book and sat back down in the chair by the window, glancing out at the snow-covered expanse, and noticed that most of the popcorn was gone from the tree. A few birds picked at the snowy ground, foraging for any missed kernels. He opened the book and slowly flipped through the pages. It seemed his entire life was chronicled within. He noticed how rarely in the pictures he'd smiled. Even as a small child, he had such a serious countenance. Moments in time that should have been joyous—birthdays, parties, holidays—did not elicit smiles from Brad. On looking at his emotionless features, it seemed almost as if he had tried *not* to smile, not to reveal his feelings at all.

There were many pictures of his mother, and he felt a pain in his heart he realized was sadness. He'd not really allowed himself to experience sadness at her funeral, banishing it away through sheer force of will. It was a painful feeling but not entirely bad. It was almost a relief to know that he could feel emotion. The sadness was accompanied by a longing, a realization that he would never see his mother again. She had loved him, had cared for him, and sacrificed for him. In all the pictures of her, especially the pictures of the two of them together, she was smiling. She was happy despite their circumstances. Intellectually, he had known times were hard for her after his father died, but she had never seemed weary or unsatisfied.

He flipped the page and saw a picture of his mother and father together. His mother was smiling serenely, but his father stared back at him with the same expressionless face Brad had exhibited in all of his pictures. It appeared that his mother had also married someone quite different from herself. He flipped through more pages, until he arrived at the last few.

There was a snapshot at their wedding with Ellie gazing at him, happy and content, and Brad looking tense. He remembered the day and remembered feeling happy. Why couldn't he *look* happy? How selfish was his heart that he could not express his gratitude for a loving wife and a life others could only dream of?

He flipped the next page and saw a piece of paper folded in two and slipped into the photo slot in the album page. He carefully pulled the album page apart and slid the paper out. He opened the paper to reveal a black and white image with dates and numbers. After a few minutes, he realized it was an ultrasound image. At the top of the page were Ellie's name, date of birth, and the date *December 20*. He could not believe what he was seeing. He was stunned, amazed, yet elated. His heart was pounding in his chest. He could feel his mouth curling into the most outrageous grin. He rubbed his palms over the paper, and then held it up in front of his face just to confirm what he was seeing and that it was real.

He looked at Ellie's name, with his last name, astonished that she was his wife and that she was carrying his child. His love for her welled up inside of him and tears spilled out of his eyes, although the outrageous grin on his face was still present. He jumped up from his chair and spun around, not knowing what to do next. He wanted to go to Ellie, wake her up, hold her in his arms and thank her, kiss her, promise her his love, his life, his very best. But then he did not want to wake her. She needed her sleep. She was going to be a mother! He wanted to scream and dance and run around the room. He wanted to celebrate! He glanced out the window at the incredible winter's day in absolute joy.

The Christmas present that had been such a disappointment had held the most astonishing gift, and Ellie had chosen such a thoughtful way to reveal the gift, allowing him to discover it in his own time. After his behavior yesterday, had she wondered if she'd made a mistake? Was she afraid that he would be unhappy about the baby or, worse yet, angry? Could he ever show her how much he loved her?

Today felt like it was the first day of his life, his new life. He didn't know if the grin would ever leave his face. Happiness and contentment and fulfillment glowed inside his chest like a bright coal of fire. He glanced out the window to see the sun shining on the crisp blanket of snow, glittery, blazing white, making the world bright and new.

It was the most glorious of days.

About the author:

Vickie Clasby resides in Franklin, Tennessee with her husband, twelve-year-old daughter, ten-year-old twin sons, two cats and a crazed Husky mix dog. She works as a business analyst for a major healthcare company. Her life is filled with corporate drama, domestic chaos, and endless writing material. Vickie has written several short stories, essays, and a mystery novel, and is currently working on a sequel. "The Most Glorious Day" is her first published work.

THE ENCOUNTER
©2008 by Robyn Wicks

His eyes wandered around the room and came to rest on the woman sitting alone in the corner. He leaned back in the chair, made himself comfortable and studied her. She was not beautiful or pretty. His mind searched for a word to describe her. He settled on pleasant; a pleasant face without guile. She had an air of refinement about her, and a long, black, ankle-length dress, accompanied by a black lace shawl draped loosely over her shoulders added an air of mystery. *Class,* he thought, *the woman has class.* He continued his observations. She wore a gold ankh on a gold chain around her neck, simple and elegant. Her hands rested quietly in her lap and he could see a ring glittering as it caught the light from the lamp on the table beside her.

She rose from the chair and walked across to the bar to refresh her drink. His eyes followed her body as it moved under the dress, and he imagined the black gown slipping from her body, revealing firm breasts and long legs. He shifted uncomfortably and grinned to himself. *Nice,* he thought, *very nice.*

He watched her as she poured the soft drink into her glass. *A non-drinker, that's interesting,* he thought. As she returned to her chair, his eyes followed her, roving the length of her body, stirring desires. She settled herself into the chair and glanced around the room, meeting his eyes for a moment and quickly lowering her gaze, focusing on the glass in her hand. Having observed her overall appearance, he focused his attention on her face. He revised his earlier appraisal. *She is attractive,* he thought.

Brown, medium length hair framed a calm face, bearing a hint of makeup deftly applied and accentuating her eyes. *I wonder what colour her eyes are,* he thought. *Her lips are perfect,* he mused, the lipstick a soft, subtle shade far sexier than a slash of bright red.

She glanced at her wristwatch, and he sensed her desire to make the hands on the watch move faster. A woman approached her with a tray of snacks. She smiled and accepted the offer, taking a cracker with cheese.

Wow, he thought, *what a beautiful smile. It lights up her whole face.* A noise across the room caught his attention and he looked towards the commotion. He watched for a few moments, but nothing interesting followed, and his gaze returned to the woman. She was staring at him. *Ah,* he thought, *I am being quietly studied.* He smiled. Instantly she averted her eyes and concentrated on the carpet beneath her feet. *Her eyes,* he thought, *what colour are her eyes? And I wonder what her name is. Is she here alone? Is she waiting for someone? Married? I wonder what she is thinking, sitting there alone in the corner.*

"I need some answers" he said softly. He stood up, reached for his empty glass and wandered over to the bar.

***

I wish he would stop staring at me, she thought, *I feel bad enough just being here, let alone having someone stare at me.* Not feeling confident enough to make eye contact, she had not had a chance to study him. A brief glance when she returned with a fresh drink had given her limited information on her admirer. Tall, sandy blonde hair, very good looking—she would go as far as handsome—and well dressed was all she had been able to absorb with the brief glance she had allowed herself before she found herself under his intense scrutiny.

She studied the glass in her hands. *Why does he keep staring at me?* she wondered. *There are plenty of women here, some of them quite beautiful. Why is he looking at me?* She glanced at her wristwatch. *I just want to go home,* she thought. *So many people, I just want to go home.* A tray appeared in front of her. Not wanting to appear rude, she took a cracker and slice of cheese, smiling at the woman offering her the food.

A noise across the room caught his attention and she took the opportunity to observe him. Blue jeans accentuated his long legs, and the black sweater contrasted beautifully with his sandy blonde hair. *I wonder what colour his eyes are,* she thought. *I cannot see them from this distance. He is strikingly handsome, and what a beautiful smile. Oh no, he is staring at me again.* She lowered her eyes and stared at the carpet. *His eyes are dark, I am sure of it,* she thought. *Green or brown. I wonder what he is thinking. I wonder if he is here with someone. He has such a nice smile. What if he comes over and talks to me?*

She raised her eyes and glanced around the room. She saw him stand and her eyes followed him as he walked across the room toward the bar, dodging people, smiling and answering "Hi" to people he passed. He stopped to talk to a group of men and women. She watched him as he interacted with his peers. *How confident he is,* she thought, *how relaxed and easy going.* "I wish I had such confidence," she whispered. The room suddenly felt oppressive, closing in on her. *I need some fresh air,* she thought and her eyes scanned the room, seeking an escape route.

***

As he walked towards the bar he saw a colleague and his wife.

"Hi, Mike. Didn't think you were coming," said his friend.

"Hi. I wasn't, but I figured why not, nothing better to do."

"Mike, this is my wife Sarah. Sarah, Mike".

"Hi," she said. "Nice to finally meet you."

"Nice to meet you, Sarah. Well, you were right about one thing, Frank." he said.

"Oh?" said Frank, cocking his head to one side. "What?"

"You are married to a beautiful lady."

Frank grinned. "Sure am," he said happily.

Sarah smiled, looking at her husband adoringly. "Thank you, Mike."

"Perhaps you two can help me out. Any chance you know the name and details of the lady sitting over there in the far corner by the lamp?" he said.

"What lady? Where?"

He turned and looked in the direction of his desire. "Damn," he whispered. "Damn, damn, damn. Where the hell did she get to?"

***

The glass door that led to the balcony was slightly ajar. She stepped out onto the balcony and felt the cool night air dance across her skin. Walking towards the railing she looked up at the magnificent full moon. She smiled. Of all the things in this world, she loved the full moon most.

There was something mysterious, magical about a full moon. Moonlight and starlight. Magic. A soft laugh caught her attention and she glanced at the corner of the balcony. In the shadows she could see the outline of two people locked in an embrace. She averted her gaze, not wanting to disturb their moments together, and moved along the balcony away from the noise of the party. Walking down the marble steps, she found herself in a garden. The smell was delicious. Roses.

"I wonder what his name is," she said to the roses. "I wonder what colour his eyes are."

"It's Mike, and they are green."

Startled, she jumped and a small cry escaped her lips.

"Sorry," he said. "Should have known coming up behind you and speaking would be unsettling. Took me awhile to find you. What brings you out here away from the party?"

"I don't like crowds," she said softly.

He walked towards her. She stepped back, as if wary of him. He stopped, sensing her fear. "Would you like to go back up onto the balcony in sight of the crowd?" She nodded. He stepped aside and bowed dramatically, grinning. "This way, my dear." She hurried past him, eyes downcast. He sighed. *This is going to be hard work*, he thought.

She reached the safety of the balcony and was about to enter the room.

He spoke softly behind her. "Please don't. I really am harmless. Won't you stay out here and talk with me for a while?"

She hesitated. Thoughts danced inside her head, waging a mini war. *He seems nice. I should go inside.*

Why? Why not take a chance for once in your life?

He will get bored with me very quickly.

Then what's the problem? He gets bored, he leaves. Simple. At least you would have taken that first step.

"Okay," she whispered.

"Great. First-things-first. May I know your name?"

"It's Maria."

"A beautiful name. Hello, Maria."

"Hello."

The balcony door burst open and the voice of a very drunk woman shattered the moonlit calm. "Maria. *Mariiiiiiaaaaaaaaaaaaaa!* Oh, there you are. Dave wants to go home. Come on. He is sober enough to drive, so we are leaving now."

"I can drive you home," said Mike, desperate not to lose her before he got to know her. "Not a good idea to go with anyone who has been drinking and intends to drive."

"I don't know you," she said warily.

"Sure. But I can fix that easily. Stay. Talk to me for awhile. If you decide you don't like me, I will ring a taxi for you. You have my word. You can trust me."

She looked at her friend, swaying unsteadily on her feet, and for the first time in her life stepped out onto the limb. "Ok. I will stay and talk to you."

He grinned. "This way, my lady," he said, leading her down the steps to the polished wooden bench in the garden. "Make yourself comfortable, and I shall return with refreshments." He smiled and wandered back up the steps to the balcony door.

She knew it was coming and she took a deep breath to calm herself. She looked up at the moon and closed her eyes, absorbing the moonlight, letting its magic seep into her skin, filling her with its power. "Mother Moon, I hear your call" she whispered, her hands moving in an ancient ritual. "I feel your power." She chanted softly, the words old and powerful. It was during this time, the beginning of the ritual, that she felt the power rise inside her, the power that shackled the quiet, shy, gentle Maria, and allowed the transformation to occur. She felt strong, her blood coursing with the spirit of her ancestors and a servant to the call of the Moon.

***

As Mike reached the doorway he turned and looked back at the woman sitting on the bench. She had her back to him, and the moonlight gave her hair a wondrous glow. Sensing that there was something special about her, he had an overwhelming desire to sit and talk to her and, if Lady Luck was kind to him, get to know her more intimately. *I have a feeling that tonight will be very interesting*, he thought.

"Coke, right?" Mike said as he sat down beside her and handed her a glass.

"Yes. Thank you." She smiled shyly and took the glass from him, letting her hand come into contact with his for a moment.

"It's a beautiful night, isn't it? I love nights like this when the moonlight washes over the land and gives everything a...I don't know...a kind of mysterious, ghostly feeling" he said.

They sat in the garden talking for almost an hour, light banter that put them at ease in each other's company.

"You were correct," she said.

"About?"

"Trusting you. I feel as though I can trust you."

"Why, thank you, my lady," he grinned.

"Would you do something for me, please? I know that I should not take liberties with a friendship that is but an hour old, but you can always say no, and nothing will be lost".

"Name it."

"It is such a beautiful night. I do not wish to go home so early. There is a place I know of, not far from here. Would you be so kind as to take me there? If you love the moonlight as I do, I will show you a sight that will fill your senses with wonder."

"To my carriage, my lady," he replied enthusiastically.

***

They walked through the trees and entered a small clearing illuminated by the moonlight. A large, circular rock dominated the clearing.

"Breathtakingly beautiful," Mike said softly.

"Come, lay on the rock with me," she said.

"Not my first choice of a place to lay with you, but hey, lead me to it," he laughed. *I wonder why my hand feels so odd*, he thought.

Mike tried to fight the dizziness, tried to fight the desire to slip into darkness.

She chanted the ancient words of power softly, her head back and her arms outstretched.

***

Detective Inspector Franklin stared at the body. He had seen a lot in his twenty-seven years as a police officer, but murder scenes like this always got to him. "What would possess a human being to do such a thing to a fellow human being?" he muttered.

"Ritual killing. Seems to have been only one person here, besides the victim, of course," replied his partner who had come to stand next to him.

"There is not a part of him without a mark, without a slash."

"Yeah, a knife will do that in the right hands. Any sign of the heart?"

"No, and I have a feeling there won't be. Poor bastard."

"Yep. He joins the other four poor bastards. Let's hope this one has some ID."

***

He watched her as she walked over to the table and sat down. She picked up the menu and began to read. *I wonder what her name is*, he thought.

About the author:

Robyn Wicks lives in Nowra, New South Wales, Australia. She is a high school History and English teacher and has been teaching for 10 years. She came to teaching late in life, starting university when she was 44 years old. She has two children: son Che is 32 and daughter Kym is 29. She has four beautiful granddaughters: Shannon (9), Lorien (7), Ella (2 1/2), and Erin (6 months). Writing short stories is a new adventure for her as she has only been writing for about three years. She enjoys reading, tapestry, and online chat.

HEAVEN ON EARTH
©2008 by Kathleen E. Fitzpatrick

Black. The world had gone black. There was no tomorrow. There was no future. There was nothing. And I didn't care. I had it all. It was all gone. I could scream until my lungs ripped. I could cry until my tear glands dried up. Nothing would change. Nothing-nothing-nothing-nothing-NOTHING. My greatest fear had been realized, and it was more awful than I could have ever imagined.

One week ago, I woke up to the sweet sounds of my son's four-year-old voice singing "The Itsy-Bitsy Spider" over the baby monitor. Like the unappreciative soul that I was, I grumbled as I rolled out of bed in a bleary-eyed stupor. I walked into his bright yellow room. Even my drowsiness couldn't muffle the joy that bubbled up in me every time I saw him. I always found myself enchanted by his chubby, pink face; his plump, little mouth; and his big, bright blue eyes lined with the kind of lashes only little boys are blessed with. It always seemed that some kind of dazzling energy came from inside him and sparkled through those brilliant eyes.

After having Cheerios with bananas for breakfast and watching Sesame Street, we got dressed for our daily trip to the park. After our shoes were on, we headed out. I let him walk by himself on the sidewalks, but he had to hold my hand as we crossed the street. I always held his hand a little tighter than necessary. We crossed the first street quickly.

When we came to the second street, a four-way intersection, I instinctively reached down to pick him up. "Aidan, Mommy will carry you across this street," I told him.

"No, NO!" He fought with me. "I want to hold hands, Mommy!"

I sighed. I still felt like I needed to hold him. "Okay," I conceded, unable to hold the weight of his small, strong body as he thrashed against me trying to get down. We carefully looked both ways.

"Is it okay, Mommy?"

The rule was that he had to ask Mommy before he crossed a street, even though we were holding hands. "Yes," I replied and we started across.

I never saw it coming. I would replay that moment in my mind over and over. I had said, "Yes." He trusted my experience and street-crossing expertise to keep him safe and I had said "Yes, cross the street." I had been wrong.

Dead wrong.

The pick-up truck came from behind us and hung a left without stopping. I didn't hear the beast until it was too late. A streak of gray was all I saw as I felt my son ripped from my hand, and a blinding pain shoot through the right side of my body.

For only an instant, I lay in the street in physical pain, grasping to understand what had happened. Then it hit me. "Aidan!" I screamed as I rolled to my left side, I could see him lying on the ground. *Oh, God,* I prayed, *Oh God please don't let him be hurt.*

I knew though. He was just lying in the street. I crawled over to him on my left hand and knee, dragging my right leg behind me. "No, no, no...please...please..."

When I got to him, he was making a soft whimpering noise. "Mommy," he whispered.

"I'm here," I said, kissing his little forehead and trying to figure out what to do first. There was blood on his head. There was blood everywhere. As I tried desperately to figure out where the blood was coming from, a woman in a blue SUV screamed out her window, "I'm calling 911!"

"Mommy," Aidan said again softly.

"I'm here, baby. It's going to be okay," I said. I lifted him into my lap to comfort him and held him close to me. His blue eyes were looking up at me, and then they fluttered and began to close. "Aidan!" I shrieked. His blue eyes opened again. "Stay with me honey, help is coming."

He moaned quietly.

"What hurts, angel? Your head?"

"Yeah," he said softly "And my tummy, my back."

The physical pain of a broken arm, leg, and two ribs was quickly surpassed by the unbearable torture of not being able to make his suffering go away. "Help is coming, honey." His eyes fluttered again. "Aidan!" I screamed again. "Don't leave me. Mommy loves you, baby. Mommy loves you so much. *Oh, God! Help us!*

His eyes opened sleepily. "I love you, too, Mommy," he said in that soft, unfamiliar tone.

I glanced at the SUV; the woman was talking frantically on her cell phone. In the distance, I saw the emergency lights of an ambulance. "Look, honey, a fire truck," I said hoping he would perk up a little more. He just stared up at me. I held his gaze, kissing him once more.

All at once, paramedics descended upon us. He was ripped from my hands once more. I tried to follow the paramedics to the van. "Ma'am," said an older paramedic, "we need to treat *your* injuries as well."

"Do it at the hospital. I want to ride with my son."

"I understand, ma'am, but we don't know the extent of your injuries."

"NO!" I screamed, "I am riding with him. Help me into the van."

"You'll have to sign this release that says you refused treatment at the scene," the paramedic began to explain.

"Give it to me, I am going with my son."

In the ambulance, Aidan was strapped to a backboard. There was such a flurry of activity, it was difficult to tell what was going on. "Stay awake, buddy," the paramedics kept saying.

I was lying next to him holding his hand. I leaned over to look at him, he said nothing, but he held my gaze all the way to the hospital. "I love you so much," I kept whispering to him. I would be told later that he had gone into shock. This detail about my child's death was supposed to make me feel better because it meant that he had not suffered. It did, but not much.

***

My husband met us at the emergency room and went with Aidan.

"I am going to give you a sedative, Mrs. Scott," the nurse told me. Apparently, I had begun screaming.

I don't know how long I had been at the hospital before my husband came to my recovery room. I had asked the attending nurse about Aidan. She said she would find out. She never came back.

When my husband did walk in the door, I knew. The look on his face told me everything. I would have given my own heart to be wrong.

"Aidan?" I asked hopefully, fearfully.

He couldn't say the words. He didn't need to. Tears streamed down his cheeks.

"No," I sobbed, rocking back and forth. My hands were grasping, trying to bring Aidan back, trying to push all of this away like a bad dream, trying to grab some cure, some hope. But, there was nothing that could fix this and there was no hope. There was nothing. I vomited.

My husband had asked the doctors to wait to take Aidan's body away. He brought me to my limp, heaven-bound angel. I held his cold little body for the last time. I sobbed and sobbed. No "extra" time was enough. It would have to end. I would have to let him go. I would have to plan his funeral. I would have to bury him.

"I'm so sorry, baby. I love you with all my heart." I just kept talking to him and kissing him, irrationally hoping that no one would interrupt me as long as I was talking. I don't know how long

I held him. It didn't matter. It wasn't enough. When one of the nurses finally did apologetically tell me it was time to go, I nodded silently and looked down at my little boy, once so full of energy and life, bruised and limp in my arms. "Goodnight, sweetheart. I love you."

Over the next few days, the grief rippled out from us as we notified family and friends, a job of which my stricken parents generously relieved us. My husband and I made funeral plans in alternating states of quiet agony and discordant hysterics.

The day before the wake, a detective and an assistant district attorney arrived at our door. They had found the driver. He had a suspended license from a previous DUI, and there were empty beer bottles in the cab of his murderous pick-up truck. He was in custody.

All my grief, the enormous pain in my heart, the sickness in my stomach, turned to anger in a blinding fury. I wanted to kill. I wanted to torture this man. I wanted blood. I wanted him to suffer the way my baby had, the way my husband and I would suffer for the rest of our lives. Rotting in jail was too good for him. He ripped my child from my hands. He extinguished a bright, beautiful life full of happiness and hope. He left my baby broken and dying in the street and he didn't even stop. I was consumed by hate.

The assistant district attorney explained that I would be called as a witness in his trial and that we would both be asked to give victim impact statements. We pledged to help them in every way that we could. They gave their condolences and left.

Alone in Aidan's room, I teetered on the rim of insanity. Part of me did want to kill this man, part of me wanted to kill myself. I don't know what made me pull out my grandmother's old rosary. I hadn't even looked at it since it came in the small box of jewelry and other items I'd inherited when she passed. Hoping for I don't know what, a miracle maybe, I closed my eyes and prayed. I prayed each Hail Mary and Our Father. I felt some of the pain of this world fade as I lay upon Aidan's fire engine toddler bed. As I grasped each bead, cruel reality seemed to take a step back. I was with Aidan. It was as if I dove into that deep, black abyss in my heart, the space that used to be Aidan's, and I was there. I don't know where, but I was with Aidan. The energy of those bright blue eyes rushed through me. I felt his soft breath on my cheek. I felt his hand in mine.

I was with a woman who had suffered what I was suffering, a mother who understood my agony. I focused my prayers on my son. For a moment, a soft comfort washed over me. The comfort that comes with knowing your child is safe and happy. In the night of my mind, I knew that when I opened my eyes the pain and anger would still be waiting, but here in this dark place, I could find some relief from this living nightmare.

At the wake, I sat next to Aidan's small coffin. He was dressed in his little Easter suit. I kept one hand on his cold head and stroked his hair as family and friends prayed, kissed his little forehead and passed in varying depths of grief and sympathy. Tomorrow, I knew that I would have to do the unthinkable.

Now here I stand in the midst of a black, mourning sea. It is time to close his small coffin. I will never see my beautiful baby again. I place the small rosary Aidan received at his baptism in his casket. I lean in and kiss both of his cheeks, his forehead and his tiny hands. My husband does the same. Our tears run down Aidan's cheeks.

The funeral director motions us back and closes the small coffin. My husband and I cling to each other and wail. The world has gone black with death.

With my head buried in my husband's jacket and my rosary in my hand, I hear a woman's soft voice, "He's right here." My heart skips a beat and I feel an umbilical pull telling me that we are connected. That connection won't take away my pain. It won't give me my son back. But it will be enough. It will be that glimmer of hope in my most desperate hours. It will help me out of bed each morning. It will give me the ability to go on. The path I am left to journey will not be the one I anticipated, but I will travel it still. I will travel holding my son safely in my grieving heart. I will travel it with mothers who share my unspeakable suffering. I will go on through this nightmare.

I will go on through this hell because, every so often, I get a glimpse of heaven.

About the author:

Kathleen E. Fitzpatrick works in communications and fundraising in Illinois. "Heaven on Earth" is her first work to be published. She has a wonderful, loving family whom she tries to spend as much time with as possible. Kathleen is especially grateful to her husband, Casey, who has given her the gift of time to discover her writing talents.

MIND THE GAP
©2008 by Atossa Shafaie

MIND THE GAP. Mary stared at the white words on the platform until they went blurry. Her wiry legs dangled over her bags, tucked away under the bench to keep from interfering with London's busiest morning hour. She began to realize why her ticket back home was so cheap. Getting to Heathrow would be a nightmare! Morning commuters wrapped their anxiety around themselves as they shuffled on and off trains. Barely anyone looked up from magazines, palm pilots or novels.

Mary always tried to see what people were reading. What people chose to spend their unassigned moments on could, she believed, give her some small insight to the pair of eyes skidding across the pages. More than once, they would catch her staring, and she would always say "hi", in hopes of starting a conversation. Rarely did it ever happen.

Richard had been an exception. Many years ago, Mary traveled to Scotland, and found herself standing beside him, waiting for the public bus in front of the battlefield of Culloden. Richard had his nose buried in a book. He wore oversized khaki shorts, a button-down, pastel-colored, short sleeve shirt, and some very strange looking but seemingly comfortable shoes. His brow was crinkled and his glasses were sliding down a very perfect nose.

She leaned a bit closer, stretching her eyes as far as they would go without obviously interfering. *The Songs of Ossian.* Was he a musician? No, he didn't look like a musician.

Before she could form her next thought, his thick Scottish drawl interrupted, "Can I help you with something?" His eyebrow was cocked and loaded, but there was a smile on his lips.

They had remained great friends since that day. Richard was not, she soon learned, a musician. He had been studying to become a barrister, at which he had become very successful. Two years ago, he moved to London, hoping to save the world, or make a great profit trying, whichever came first. So, she would visit once a year, and get away from the cultural void of America.

Mary dug into her bag and found the Cadbury Flake bar she had been saving for later. Her cell phone rang. After emptying the entire contents of her carryon across the tube station floor, she finally found it.

"Hi, Richard," she said, almost dropping the phone. "Miss me already?"

"As if I have a choice," he teased. "You forgot your book here."

Mary rifled through the stuff on the floor. "Which one?"

"Some ridiculous book with fear in the title."

"Oh, yeah, *Feel Fear and Do It Anyway*. It's a good book, you should read it."

Richard laughed on the other end. "I don't feel fear. Why the hell are you reading it?"

Mary put her stuff back in order, balancing the cell phone between her ear and shoulder. "Hello? How quickly we forget! I am afraid of flying."

"And that book is supposed to cure you? Brilliant."

"No, the Ambien cures me, usually within five to ten minutes. The book is supposed to make me feel better about being afraid in the first place."

"I don't know what's worse, this self-help nonsense or that bible you carry around with you. What about God, don't you think he'll be offended that you don't trust him a bit more?"

A train rolled off behind her, generating a breeze flavored with dank tunnel smells. Mary shivered. "God forgives me. That's how it works Richard. I sin, go to confession, and God forgives me. If you weren't so against anything holy, you would know that."

"Religious, I'm against anything religious," Richard corrected. "Not the same thing at all."

Mary pulled on her sweatshirt, somehow managing to keep the cell phone in place. Her thin, blond hair rose up, seeking out the static in the air. She smoothed it down and resettled herself. Another train grumbled through, and she ignored it.

"Last chance to come back with me, sure you won't take me up on it?"

"As tempting as the land of bikini contests and *Amish in the City* is, I think I'll pass."

Mary shook her head. She was smiling, though she didn't know it. "I took you to *one* bikini contest. I thought you'd find it interesting in a National Geographic sort of way. And we saw *Amish in the City* here on your TV. I'd never even heard of it until then."

Richard had, in an unprecedented move, surprised her by stopping over in D.C. on his way back from India. Mary thought the comparison between Sterling, VA and the Taj Mahal was a rather unfair one. Had it not been for Maryam, the whole thing would have been a disaster. Her best friend was a beautiful, far too smart Persian girl who swept the uncapturable Richard away with her smile. She was Muslim, he was not, so nothing serious would ever come of it. But Mary had secretly thanked God that she had something other than tourist traps and sports bars to offer! Who knows what might have happened between them if he had not been forced to leave early. His mother fell ill and he flew out on September ninth, 2001. Richard had not been back since.

"Call me when you get there, and tell Maryam I said hi."

"Tell her yourself," Mary teased.

"Be nice. I'll talk to you later."

"Absolutely."

Two trains had come and gone while she spoke to Richard. Mary wasn't in a rush. The very thought of getting one step closer to an airport where she would be forced to take the walk of doom down a flimsy, extended corridor and onto a plane made her stomach lurch. She began biting her nails. Her bracelet stroked her cheek and she examined it with a smile.

"Take it," Maryam had said. "And wear it all the time. It will keep you safe."

Maryam's grandmother had been making them more food. And inevitably, Mary would eat it to the last bite. No human could resist Papi's cooking. The spices gently reminded her of places she had never seen: hot summer nights amidst ripe pomegranate trees, fields of sunflowers. The rice was fluffy and soft, its own texture, and the *Tadig*, Mary's favorite, was the crunchy, hard-burnt layer of rice at the bottom of the pan. Without fail, before she served it, Papi would apologize for the less than perfect meal, which was indeed always perfect, and wait for the expected contradictory compliments.

Maryam's mother was burning rue for Mary, another act of protection. Apparently, the smoky, soily smell of dried rue as it burned kept the evil eye away. The evil eye was very big in Maryam's culture. Maryam gave Mary the silver charm bracelet in a beautiful pouch of colored material. She had brought it back from Iran and was saving it for just the right moment. It was a hand, palm outward, with an eye in the center of it. Maryam promised Mary that if she never took it off, she would make it home just fine.

Her hair smelled of jasmine, and Mary could remember dark, long, perfect curls pushing against her face as her best friend hugged her. It had been fifteen years since Mary had walked up to the new girl in school and introduced herself. They had been instantly inseparable.

"You are Muslim?"

The deep cadence of a stranger's question snapped Mary out of her remembrances. He was a handsome African-American. Well, not American, his accent was clearly British.

"You are Muslim?" he repeated.

Mary followed his gaze to her wrist. "Oh no, no. I am not

Muslim. My good friend back home is. She gave this to me because I'm afraid of flying. It's for protection."

The man arched his brow and shifted his backpack to the other shoulder. "Do you know what we call it?" he asked.

"She told me it was the Hand of Fatima," Mary answered.

"Very good," the man said and smiled. "Also known as the Khamsa."

His eyes met hers, and she shivered. They were deep and clear and for a moment, a flutter of recognition passed through them.

She showed him the gold crucifix around her neck. "I'm Catholic," she offered. Her crucifix was handed down, from grandmother to mother to her. "Every Sunday, church."

Mary immediately felt the space between them grow cold.

"Then you should trust in your God and not be afraid for your life."

It was a common argument but somehow not comforting when Mary envisioned dangling thirty-two thousand feet above ground.

"Of course you are right. But I'm sure that is what all the people on all the planes crashes thought," she answered half-jokingly.

The man smiled and Mary thought she saw a veil of a secret in it. "And your god doesn't mind that you wear a Muslim charm?"

Mary grew silent. "There's only one God," she said. "And I think he sees The Hand of Fatima as I do, a beautiful gift to keep me safe."

The man seemed surprised. The train rattled down the track. "You are American?" he asked, trying to hide an accusation.

"Yes," she said defensively.

The man looked at the ground, mumbling something inaudible. There was a strange pulse in his voice. The hair on Mary's arms prickled.

"Going to Heathrow?" he finally asked.

"Yes," she answered and, without thinking, started biting her nails again. There was a short pause, and the rumbling of their train sounded from deep inside a dark tunnel.

"I heard today, on my way here, that the train to Heathrow is not running. You'll have to take a cab at some point anyway, better do it now and save yourself the time."

Richard had not mentioned anything about the trains. He was a news addict and never missed a hit in the morning. She didn't want to be rude and contradict the man. She actually didn't want to be near him at all. So, with a sigh of relief that confused her, she thanked the stranger's back as he squeezed his way onto the train along with hundreds of strangers on their way to life and another day.

Mary didn't want to wait for the next train. The thought of having to sit amidst all those people as they intruded on her private fear festival exhausted her. And, having waited around too long at King's Cross, she might miss the plane if the man had been right about trouble with the trains.

Mary sighed, and grabbed her things, dreading the long haul back to the street. She hailed a black taxi and dragged her bags on behind her.

"Where to, Luv?"

"Heathrow."

"All the way?" the cabbie asked surprised.

"Since the trains aren't working, I don't have much of a choice, do I?" Mary hoped she had enough pounds left for the ride.

"I never heard anything about the trains, but all the way it is."

She sat back and wondered if she packed her Ambien in an easy to find place.

***

They informed her at Scotland Yard that the man who had spoken to her was a terrorist. That the backpack she had paid no attention to carried explosives. Twenty minutes after he boarded the train, he took his own life, along with twenty-six others. It *would* have been twenty-seven. It *should* have been.

Mary went cold. They said he saved her because she must have reminded him of his wife. They showed Mary a picture, and it was true, she did look like his wife, his pregnant wife. He was

Jamaican born, but raised in England. His mother and he both converted to Islam. His wife was a Brit who did the same.

They rambled on with facts and questions and she drifted further away. It didn't matter to her where he was born, or who he was.

After it was all done with, every stone unturned, every question neatly put away, Mary was left alone in a room to "compose herself." Mary didn't know where to begin. She sat in silence, biting her nails and crying.

She remembered the strength in her mother's arms as they nearly embraced the breath out of her. "Thank God you are safe! I have gone to church and given alms. Thank God, thank God!"

It was Allah that Maryam gave her thanks to. She had attributed Mary's safekeeping to the charm. After all, he wouldn't have talked to her if not for the Hand of Fatima. It became a very important fact to Maryam, who had been put, in the last few years, in the repeated position of having to defend Islam, and explain that not all Muslim's believed in terrorism. Not all Iranians hated America. She could manage being a good Muslim and loving America at the same time.

Mary felt a strange tug of war begin in her life. God, Allah, she was a prize both sides wanted credit for. She went to church, sat in the pew and thanked God. For the first time ever, it was an empty gesture, void of shape or form. She knew the truth. A *man* had decided.

The priest had revered her as if she were some sacred thing he was afraid to touch. "God has saved you," he said with his best sermon voice. "You were in the presence of evil, and God kept you from it."

"Where was God when that evil took the twenty-six people who did die?" she asked.

"Child, you must never question God's will. He will always know what is best."

She looked around her at the gilded worship of Jesus, the pious silence of God's place. That silence could not live in her anymore.

She had lost weight she could not afford to be rid of, and her face had become a grey shadowy thing void of sleep. When she shut her eyes, she saw his.

The crucifix around her neck felt heavy. Everyone was so relieved, so happy, but all she could hear was the question that plagued her: "Why me?"

She thought of the wife, the one she must have reminded him of, the baby that was waiting to be born, the one that would never know its father, or might get to know him as a murderer, a monster, maybe even a hero.

"What was he like?" Her aunt had asked her, wide- eyed.

"Excuse me?" she whispered. It was the thing everyone wanted to talk about most. What was the terrorist like, what kind of man could do what he did? They wanted to hear about a monster. How could she answer? Pedophiles don't have two heads, rapists don't have horns, and terrorists don't look any different than you or I. They don't sound any different. At least this one didn't.

"It all happened so fast. I only talked with him for two minutes. I don't know what he was like."

What was I like, she would wonder, that he kept me off that train? Had she been an inexplicable hiccup in his finite world of monotheistic manipulation? What could he have thought of a young woman who wore a Muslim charm and a Catholic one on the same body?

But it was Richard that gave the explanation that fit most comfortably. Perhaps it was just a case of seeing in her the reflection of the woman that he loved as his wife. Perhaps, Mary was to him just a person, someone worth saving.

"If only," Richard had whispered, "we could all always see everyone that way."

His hug had been the most healing of all, he who didn't have a side to pull her to. And maybe that is why she had come back here against the wishes of her family and friends. She hoped she could find her silence somewhere between Richard's wisdom and the place where her life was spared. Standing at the same spot, she looked up at the arches, still there, still ignored, still beautiful. Around her, people moved on, and whether they forgot, or paused in memory, whether they refused to fear, or felt hesitation, they showed nothing. Mary was no longer interested in what they read.

As Mary stood there without any ceremony, she slowly understood. She could wonder all she wanted, she could thank God, or let it be Allah that took credit for her, it would make no difference, and it would bring her no answers. God wasn't speaking to her, Allah wasn't watching. What happened that day was not borne of divine intervention. It was Maryam's belief in the Hand of Fatima, it was her own faith in the crucifix, but more than just these things, it was her inability to see the man that spoke to her as a threat, her instinct to answer him, to interact with him.

It's how she met all the important people in her life, by talking to strangers, exactly as she was taught never to do. Richard had been right. They were, for one short while, just two people, and that had changed his mind about her. The world would see it differently. Its soul could not carry the belief that a man like him could have a moment like that. And so, it would continue to go on.

Mary sat down on the bench and put her head in her hands. Through tears, her eyes caught the warning laid out before her. *MIND THE GAP.* Mary stared at the white words on the platform until they went blurry.

About the author:

Atossa was born in Tehran, Iran. The revolution caused her family to move to London, England and then to the United States. She has a B.A in English Literature from George Washington University and is currently working on her first manuscript entitled *Blood of Persia,* a historical fiction about Cyrus the Great, founder of the Persian Empire.

FAIR-HAIRED BOY GONE GREY
©2008 by Dan Sullivan

They say the Japanese, when they want a man to resign, will tuck him away in a naked office with nothing to do, until he can bear it no longer. It hadn't quite come to that. I did, after all, have a miniature bonsai and a government-issued wall calendar marking the days toward my retirement. Until then, I planned to go on writing memos to the wind in a sunless room near the Pentagon.

It hadn't always been that way. Once I had been the Special Assistant to the Director for Disaster Readiness, "his fair-haired boy" as the vast unwashed used to call me. Fresh from the university, I wrote the speeches and Congressional testimony—all the policy-level stuff—for America's disaster programs. I still picture with rueful fondness the smiling young man, a bit too eager and agreeable, bustling into offices, randy for data, a bit of a toothache for all.

I still picture, too, with heartache, Kirby Allbritton, my mentor and the Director. He had a weakness for 17th Century lyric poetry, and my senior paper at Georgetown happened to be on Andrew Marvell. During my job interview, Kirby and I discussed the motif of elegy in English love poetry. I quoted "To His Coy Mistress," and he hired me on the spot. Kirby, the grand old courtier from Virginia, the consummate gentleman, respectful and pleasant to all from the cleaning woman to the President's Chief of Staff.

Courtesy and gentleness would, in the end, be his undoing.

For years, under Kirby's headship, I wrote the words that convinced Congress to pay for what rising waters and termagant winds could do to America. I knew what Kirby wanted, and he always delivered my remarks with eloquence and passion. But numbers were never my strong suit, and the U.S. government, in the early 1980s, went to a trendy accounting system, beyond the reach of both Kirby and me. So Kirby brought on board an old friend's nephew, a recent graduate from the Business School at *The* University of Virginia. Barry Rutledge seemed benign enough, at first. He had a fullback's build and a politician's smile. He was immaculately groomed in Egyptian-cotton shirts and three-piece herringbone.

Within three months, Barry had organized a lunchtime Bible study. Within six, he was captain of the office softball team and had landed a sunny office next to mine. Within nine, he and Kirby were having breakfast together each morning. Within the year, Barry had donned the deputy's mantle and was signing memos to the staff *Re* appropriate business attire and the fitting use of government supplies. Not long after that, he began reviewing my drafts: at first, with rhapsodic praise; by degrees, with condescension; and, toward the end, with sarcastic jabs.

"Your prose, in this one, is a bit flacid, Boylan. It needs some oomph!"

I couldn't help myself and returned his comments with a correction of "flaccid." I added a marginal note, "Thanks, Barry. By the way, is 'oomph' part of our new editorial standard?" In retrospect, that may not have been the most sensible thing to do, but "flaccid" to a man, then in his forties, can prompt irrational behavior. Besides, I was still inspired by the delusion that I was, after all, "Kirby's man."

After that, Barry stopped speaking as we passed in the hallway, and he began returning my work with editorial outrage—bold, red marks with profuse, angry question marks and triple underscoring. I was redoing drafts three and four times a day for Barry as we approached our annual meeting with the boys at the

White House. That year, they would be evaluating our work through the impenetrable fog of zero-based budgeting. What made that year's meeting special was that the Vice President and the President's Chief Economic Advisor planned to attend. There can, after all, be great political currency in disasters.

For weeks, we prepared solely for that meeting. Kirby and Barry huddled in whispered strategy sessions, holding "murder boards," rehearsing Kirby's responses to the tough questions they were certain to ask. For my part, I drafted and re-drafted the words that Kirby would use for the jewel in the crown of his public service: a briefing of the Vice President.

Looking every bit the grand knight that morning, Kirby stood smiling at the head of the gleaming conference table; linen white hair, a butter-soft, navy-blue blazer, the crisp blue-and-red regimental tie Barry had given him for Christmas. Behind Kirby were the trappings of our month-long preparations: enlarged charts and graphs in various hues mounted on easels—the testament of our battles against the hurly-burly of Nature.

Thankfully, it was only the usual crowd from the White House that day. The Vice President and the Chief Economic Adviser had sent their regrets. Kirby got the signal to start. As he was lifting the binder with his notes, it came apart in his hands, the metallic spine, screws, and covers all clattering on the conference table. Among it all were several lurid magazines, a glossy jumble of flesh in every unspeakable position. We sat horrified, powerless to move or act. It was as if we were watching a car careen onto a crowded sidewalk. It couldn't really be happening...not at the White House...not with Kirby.

Kirby stood red-faced and confused. I removed the magazines and noticed Barry suppressing a faint smile. Barry then stood and rendered, to this day, the finest "superior subaltern" I've ever witnessed. Affecting a sweet, rueful smile at Kirby, Barry covered the points of our briefing and fielded the questions for his beleaguered and stunned superior.

Barry's behavior said to everyone on the White House staff,

"Isn't it obvious that I am a sensitive person? I have deep compassion for my superior, even if he is an old pervert, and, by the way, isn't it obvious too that I'm far more talented than any of these clowns from my agency?"

We escaped, receiving once more the imprimatur of the White House to go forth and serve the public. In the taxicab, back to the office, no one spoke, nor did anyone speak in the elevator. On the top floor in front of our suite, Kirby said softly that he wanted to speak with Barry and me in his office in an hour.

Some receive inspiration and guidance from Sacred Scripture, others from yoga and aromatherapy. I believe Barry received his during that hour from Machiavelli's *The Prince*, probably Chapter 8.

Kirby shut the door behind us and motioned us to sit. "I'm going to get to the bottom of this."

At that precise moment, Barry turned pointedly toward me. Kirby spoke quietly, if not a bit discursively, about the nobility of public service, excellence, honor, loyalty, the beauty of a moral life, the priceless worth of one's reputation. Finally, he came on point.

"I'm going to find out which one of you sabotaged me today."

Again, Barry was simply masterful. Using "sabotaged" as his cue, he turned again and looked directly at me. Kirby had nothing more to say, and we left.

Before he had gotten to "the bottom of it," and before I had made my appointment to see him, Kirby Allbritton suffered a massive heart attack and died one morning when he received calls from the White House and our personnel office.

Barry was invited by Kirby's widow to speak at the funeral. Then, in rapid succession, Kirby's temporary replacements left suddenly with their careers slightly dented after some embarrassing tidbit about the agency or its leader appeared in *The Washington Post*. The sources were always "unnamed."

Barry continued to ascend. With each advance, his arrogance stood taller. Abuse from him became the norm, and many of his insults were like lyric poetry—speech meant to be overheard by others.

At one of my last staff meetings there, Barry was discussing incentive awards. He reviewed a multi-year report and spoke to me for the benefit of all, "Boylan, your getting all these awards over the years from Kirby sort of cheapens it for the rest of us, don't you think?"

It then became fashionable in the agency to ridicule the memory of Kirby. Following Barry's lead, whenever a typo appeared in text or a column of figures didn't compute, even junior staff would remark, "Must be some of Dirty Kirby's handiwork."

Dirty Kirby! The grand, compassionate old man had been sent to his grave slandered. In memory, he was now a laughing stock.

Each day, I read the vacancy announcements at other government agencies. Sadly, none of the announcements called for an aficionado of 17th Century love poetry. But at last, my chance came to leave.

After a full-throated debate with Barry over the proper use of the serial comma, he declared that I was impossible to work with and gave me the "choice": crunch numbers in our budget office, or accept a job writing regulations in a sister agency at reduced pay. I chose the latter, and, late on a Sunday evening, I cleaned out my desk and locked the door behind me with my bonsai in hand.

***

Twenty years passed, and, on a bleary morning in November, as I was performing my daily ritual—a Starbuck's *venti latte* and *The Washington Post* at my desk—a headline trumpeted, **LARGEST FED REORG IN 30 YEARS**. The National Disaster Agency...it had a nice ring to it...new title, reorganization of all the old disaster offices, just the thing to revive a desiccated career.

But it also meant that all the old ghosts would soon be summoned from the four corners of the bureaucracy and gather under one roof. And it meant, of course, that I would probably be working again for Barry.

***

I was stumped. I needed a nine-letter word for "a tropical American wild cat." *The New York Times* crossword puzzle folded discreetly on my lap, I was doing my best "ruminating bureaucrat": affecting an intense, faraway gaze, worrying my brows, presumably "working" the problem with my colleagues. And the problem was this: A Category Five hurricane, Hurricane Danny, the largest in U.S. history, had made landfall on St. Thomas of the U.S. Virgin Islands. The island had been razed, and Danny had played no favorites. Hospitals, clinics, hotels, shacks, casinos, water and sewage treatment plants all in ruins. Straightaway, we needed to bring in about 500 disaster workers on an island with no power, no water, no housing. We also knew that all the compassion in the world, all the dedication and good intentions won't get very far on an empty stomach, with no sleep, or in the grip of dysentery. Meanwhile the clock was ticking, and thousands of desperate victims walked about dazed. The new Director was expecting an action plan within the hour.

Barry continued to savage us, demanding "creative solutions." The whole affair was vintage Barry: the hulking invasion of personal space, the booming insults, snide jabs....

On his immediate staff was a stunning Vietnamese-American woman who he had brought from his former agency. Ms. Nguyen was exquisite, with something from the Cavaliers' mistress about her: bee-stung lips, lustrous hair, an elegant disorder as she clattered into meetings late, clasping a mess of papers to her breast, disarming everyone with her smile. Writing on butcher paper, she was recording the low-wattage inspiration of our group.

"Come on, folks, we need some ideas. How about you? The guy over in the corner having a staff meeting with himself. What do you have to say?"

I had almost come up with "jagarundi" on my own before her interruption. *Staff meeting with myself indeed!* With tongue firmly in cheek, I answered her, "Oh, I guess we could always rent a cruise ship, probably at bargain basement prices, now with the hurricane and all, dock it at Charlotte Amalie Harbor in St. Thomas. We could feed and house our disaster workers right there from the ship, within easy access of our disaster centers."

Everyone sat stone-faced. Bureaucracy will do that to a sense of humor. Ms. Nguyen added in large girlish script CRUISE SHIP to the list on the flip chart. Barry and Ms. Nguyen huddled as they got word that the Director was on her way.

General (Retired) Anne Paxton, the first Director of the new National Disaster Agency, entered our operations center with a small retinue of aides. She positioned herself at the head of a long conference table, summarized the problem, and then nodded to Barry.

"Well, what's our plan?"

"We eliminated certain options, General. Setting up a base camp on St. Thomas for 500 workers would take too long. We'd have to start from scratch and we don't have time. Shuttling the workers each day from San Juan, Puerto Rico where we can set them up is simply unworkable: the runways in St. Thomas are screwed up and the cost is far too high. So, we feel the best option is to rent one of the idle cruise ships in the area and dock it at St. Thomas. We'd have a self-contained support system..."

General Paxton seemed to brighten. "Did you come up with that idea, Mr. Rutledge?"

Barry rendered his sincerest "blushing bureaucrat": head tipped slightly to one side, a wan smile pressing his mouth, eyes fastened on the carpeting, hands splayed...saying in effect: *Look, General, you and I both know I came up with this gem, but I don't want to grab all the credit in front of my staff. I'm a team player, but if you insist, yes, it was my idea.*

General Paxton's smile broadened as she leaned forward. "Well, was it your idea or not, Mr. Rutledge?"

Barry nodded slightly and said, "Yes, it was."

The general straightened. "Well, that's the most moronic suggestion I've heard in my thirty years of service."

The blood began to drain from Barry's face. In seconds, he was positively ashen.

"Have you lost your mind? Do you have any idea how the media would spin that? Cruise ship for disaster workers, my ass!"

Barry turned to me. "Actually, it was Boylan's idea."

"So now it's *his* idea."

Barry nodded.

"There are two things I won't tolerate in my managers, Mr. Rutledge: dishonesty to me and disloyalty to their staff. You've shown both."

She turned to me. "What's your take on all this?"

"Well, I believe caution is the watchword here, General."

I wouldn't call the color rising then in Barry's face exactly crimson. It was more a dark pink. I went on to describe the troubling images of what I feared would be the media's "take" on having Federal workers accommodated on a cruise ship in the wake of one of the worst hurricanes in U.S. history. I predicted how the tabloids would almost certainly feature a picture of our disaster employees, perhaps martinis in hand, hanging over the rail of a cruise ship, trimmed with Christmas lights, juxtaposed with a photo of lines of desperate black disaster victims snaking around a stucco building.

"The predictable caption of course, General, would read: CLUB FED."

"Thank you, Mr. Boylan. Mr. Rutledge, if that's the best you could come up with...this meeting is over. I'll find the answer myself. Thank you."

I stood with everyone else. General Paxton nodded to me. "Except you...I want you to stay." Alone with her aides and me, she asked, "So what's the solution?"

I explained what I felt would work. The Navy's Seventh District had its headquarters in San Juan, Puerto Rico, just 40 miles away from St. Thomas. I suggested we ask the Navy to dock one of its training vessels at the St. Thomas port to feed and house our workers while the Army Corps of Engineers built them quarters on the island.

"It takes care of our workers without bad press or political heat."

"And what do we do about Rutledge?"

"That's actually above my pay grade, General. But if I had to recommend anything...we do have an open disaster operation in Guam...."

General Paxton turned to an aide. "Call the Navy and cut Rutledge's orders."

The redemptive possibilities for Barry on Guam cheered me as I left the operations center.

Barry had squeezed into the packed elevator at the other end of the hallway. Shoulders hunched, dwarfed by those on either side, he looked positively baleful. Our eyes met, and he gave me a murderous look. As the elevator doors closed, I thought of Kirby, and he seemed to be speaking to my heart:

"...for I love you so/That I in your sweet thoughts would be forget/If thinking on me then should make you woe."

***

I wonder how Barry is making out in Guam? Ah, Guam after a typhoon...mosquitoes the size of Cornish game hens, dengue fever, liver flukes, dysentery, suffocating heat, reeking mounds of refuse...it is not your father's Bing Crosby-Bob Hope chirpy "Road to Polynesia."

By the way, I no longer mark the days on my calendar. My bonsai is doing just fine, getting enough sun from a southern exposure. I've added on the far wall several Hokusai prints from the Freer Gallery: "Red Fuji" and "Balloon Flower." Below, the tourists tramp across the Mall between the Smithsonian Castle and the National Gallery of Art.

Ms. Nguyen enters unannounced and places a demitasse of coffee next to my blank legal pad. There's a keynote address that I have to deliver at the American Bankers Association next week. "The Economics of Disaster Prevention." The words are just not coming.

I motion to the Victorian wing chair in front of my desk. It would be unseemly, so I make it a point *not* to look at Ms. Nguyen's bare crossed legs. She positions her exquisite hands on the armrests and re-crosses her stunning legs.

"Ms. Nguyen, have you ever written any speeches? Any testimony?"

She smiles.

I'll spare us any 17th Century conceits about her teeth, or her lips, or the glow of her skin. Suffice it to ask, how could anyone with half a soul not melt in her presence?

"No, but I'd love to give it a shot, Mr. Boylan."

Give it a shot, Mr. Boylan! That's the spirit, Ms. Nguyen. That's the spirit. Ah, youth! Kirby would be proud of you.

About the author:

Dan Sullivan teaches English literature and composition at St. Mary's Ryken High School in Leonardtown, Maryland. Dan has had three short stories published to date; the last placed second in the 2006 Scribes Valley Fiction contest, but he is most proud of his family—his wife Jamie, his daughter Laura, his son Mark, his two granddaughters Kyleigh and Erika, and his step-daughter Ploy who lives in Bangkok.

WAITING TO WANT
©2008 by Jean Tschohl Quinn

Prudence Lenhart had just begun the ironing. The three older children had already headed to school after having done their chores: feeding the chickens and the horse, milking the cow, filling the coal scuttle. The baby was back asleep in the cradle already, still a cooperative baby even at thirteen months. The little boy that ran around the outside of the house was supposed to be pulling weeds, but three-and-a-half was such a spirited age. The chore was just a ploy to keep him busy without Anna's help. Prudence knew that getting upset with him would not get it done any faster.

It was a Tuesday, pressing day, since Monday was always laundry day. Wednesday was sewing and mending. Thursday was rug beating. Friday was the day when she tended to the marketing and other errands. Saturday was baking day. That way Sunday had the nicest bread. The rest of the bread, wrapped tightly in two cloths each and stored in a bin, would slowly dry out until Friday night's dinner invariably included a bread pudding.

Hearing the Western Union boy's knock on the door, Prudence kept ironing, waiting for Anna to answer it. She sighed and set down the iron once she remembered that her helper was not even there that morning. Anna, a German émigré from a small farm outside of town, who helped Prudence during the week, was ill. She was a jolly girl who came used to hard work and was a wonder with the children. She went home on Saturdays as soon as the last loaves were in their pans for the final rising, and returned on

Monday morning an hour after dawn.

That past Sunday, Anna's mother stopped Prudence after church to say that her daughter had a fever and might not be able to work. Prudence, all concern and compassion, offered to send the doctor over. Anna's mother indignantly declined the offer. Prudence knew better than to insist.

The Western Union boy, no older than twelve, stood on the front stair and looked at her gravely. She handed him a coin from her apron pocket in exchange for the telegram. He turned immediately and walked back down the path, then stopped. He threw an "I'm sorry" over his shoulder and ran.

Her little boy, who had paused to watch the exchange, ran to her instinctively. She sat on the stair, gathering her skirts under her knees and opened the envelope.

PRUDENCE – TERRIBLE NEWS CONDOLENSCENSES
TROLLEY ACCIDENT EMIL KILLED STOP
BODY ON EVENING TRAIN FROM MADISON ON WED STOP
HEARTBREAK – W T SWENSON D-SEN

She puzzled over the telegram for a moment. Then pulling her son to her, she squeezed him tight. Just then, the baby inside cried out. She listened for a moment, wondering what the sound was, sighed, and rose to check on her.

Emil Lenhart had come to town fourteen years earlier to run the new bank. He had been raised in Cleveland, the son of a stonemason of some reputation, had some formal education, and had already had several years of banking experience. Emil had begun his pursuit of Prudence Snyder upon their second encounter, a church social. He was handsome enough, with a fine build and intelligent looks, but his manner and ease with people was singularly attractive to every unattached female in the county.

Their courtship was short by the prevailing standards; he had charmed her mother by speaking fluent German in private and careful English in public. He impressed her father with his clear-thinking and his well mapped out life. Both her parents also knew that Prudence's energy needed to be channeled sooner rather than later. Her innocent face combined with mischievous eyes, her modest dress coupled with her boisterous walk, the appropriateness of her pastimes along with her propensity for practical jokes made her a puzzle that could have caused her family no little embarrassment if not reined in.

It was a good match and, by the looks of things, a happy partnership, having produced five children within the twelve years of marriage, most born in late summer or early autumn. Prudence was the model of prudence and moderation even as she took on the social status of The Banker's Wife. The children, of varying degrees of obedience and intelligence, were generally likeable. That, Emil once told her, meant a great deal to him.

Emil's abilities with money, organization, and salesmanship made him a logical choice to run for local political office. He served well for a short time, when a state senator, the venerable Whittaker Theodore Swenson (Democrat), asked him to serve as an advisor on banking regulations. That honor required him to go to Madison for three weeks at a time every three months as he still had duties at the bank, in town, and at home.

He had left only days before. Now he was dead.

She sat jostling the baby on one knee and holding her son on the other. She said a prayer for strength and one for his soul and muttered *what-to-do, what-to-do* over and over again. Tears had yet to come. Without Anna there, she had no one to send to tell her parents or the children at school or the bank. The tears could wait.

She kissed both children on the tops of their heads, rose up, and walked to the front door, both tottering behind her. She turned to look at them, scooped the baby up and took the other's hand and started walking towards the bank.

As she entered the bank, Emil's assistant rose to meet her. That she had come without a hat and with the children signaled that something was very wrong. David Schiml, who had been one of her Sunday school students only ten years earlier, guided her to a chair and asked Mrs. McGill, a customer, to keep an eye on the children. Mrs. McGill harrumphed. She had only run over for a moment and her shop was left virtually unattended as Clarissa was a halfwit, she would tell anyone who would listen.

David's gratitude to Emil and fondness for Prudence caused him to snap, "Then send Clarissa over. Go. Please."

Prudence, hugging both children to her, nodded thanks to him.

He smiled helplessly, "Well, plenty of people will be available to help you now. She'll let everyone know in no time." She gave a weak smile, fully aware of Mrs. McGill's gossiping prowess. David squatted down in front of her to look directly into her eyes, "Now, tell me what's wrong."

While juggling the baby, she fumbled in the folds of her apron to retrieve the telegram and handed it to him.

He only said, "Oh dear."

Clarissa arrived, breathless.

With the little ones playing in the back of McGill's General under the compassionate eye of Clarissa, Prudence walked towards the schoolhouse. She didn't travel with quite the stride that had characterized her since her childhood. Whether that was because of the weight of the news, or the years of walking with children in tow, no onlooker could assess.

Karl Jensen rushed out of the blacksmith workshop towards her; the news was already spreading. "What's happened, Pru?"

"Can I tell you later, Karl?" she said, almost in a whimper.

"Sure. Yes'm." He touched her arm as she walked on.

***

Prudence and Karl had grown up on adjacent farms and had spent what would have seemed an inordinate amount of time together for a girl and a boy, had there been witnesses that far outside of town to make that assertion. The two families helped and depended upon each other for years. It was not untoward to them. Karl had always been the restless sort. He spent far more time looking to the horizon than necessary and preferred being alone, unless he was with Prudence.

Once Emil started keeping company with Prudence, Karl started looking *beyond* the horizon. He shocked the town when he eloped with the spoilt niece of a furniture manufacturer who had set up a small factory in town five years earlier.

This, incidentally, happened just weeks after Karl had talked the mayor's ugly daughter into a dalliance. Her pregnancy was covered up by a sudden visit to "her aunt in Milwaukee." The story was that she had a whirlwind courtship, married, had a baby, and was widowed all within less than a year. She returned a young widow, with the oldest looking two-month-old anyone had ever seen. She was married off a few years later to her second cousin in Chicago.

Karl had returned with Mercedes great with child about the same time, hat in hand, to his parent's farm to find that he was not particularly welcome there. He had some blacksmithing skills and was taken on by his uncle-by-marriage to craft special pieces for the furniture factory.

The pregnancy did not go well, as everyone in town was aware, for Mercedes was vocal in her complaints. She detested being in the podunk town. She disliked the provincial people. She distrusted the country doctor. Karl kept his nose in his work, but high-tailed it over to his folks' farm whenever he noticed that his father and brothers had come to town.

The son of Karl and Mercedes was taken from them when he was six by an outbreak of scarlet fever that swept through town. Long harangues that a *real* doctor could have saved her precious child followed. That she had insisted on her home remedies over his advice did not come up.

Karl worked hard for her uncle, who gave him a reasonable wage by the piece, but found it necessary to take on side work to augment his income sufficiently to support his wife at the level to which she was accustomed. The old blacksmith in town was grateful for the help, especially as more and more people began tinkering with machinery at the close of the nineteenth century;

wanting doohickeys, jiggers, and gadgets. He made an enviable living if not an enviable life.

Mercedes' imperious judgments regarding everyone and everything in the town left her with little sympathy for the loss of her child three years after the fact. When the doctor told her that her habit of taking laudanum was actually causing her latest illness, she cursed him. She cursed him till her last breath and expired with a lethal combination of ether that she had purloined from his bag, laudanum, and something from a mail order package. Karl, silent in his grief, continued to work hard with a vigor that was admirable.

Karl and Prudence understood each other more than most people knew. She had teased him all through their teen years, waiting for him to say something, do something, *anything*. But he'd look to the horizon in frustration. She thought that inviting the attentions of Emil Lenhart might have jarred him into action, but it hadn't worked. Instead, he eloped with that snot-nose from town. His ice blue eyes and masses of blond curls on a tall, wiry frame were gone. She had given him enough chances, so she turned her attentions to Emil in earnest. It was an autumn wedding.

Karl knew she had been dropping hints, but he wanted to see more of the world. He knew if he had kissed her even once, he'd be there forever. Mercedes had enticed him with her desire to get out of the little burg she had been forced to move to. She had dangled her bank account in front of his nose if he'd help her escape. The money hadn't gone nearly far enough with her whims and tastes driving their actions.

Emil, being a prudent man, had left Prudence and their five children with a tidy sum in the bank as well as a life insurance policy that would make the material aspects of life bearable. Emil was a good man.

Anna now stayed at the house. She felt guilty that she hadn't been there when the telegram had arrived. She would have been able to help with getting the children home, notifying Prudence's family, informing Mr. Schiml. She'd not leave the Lenhart family again, especially with Prudence so distracted. Well, perhaps on a Sunday afternoon if Mr. Schiml were to ask.

Anna helped Prudence ready the children for church two weeks after the wake and funeral, a wake attended by virtually everyone in the county. Karl tipped his hat as Prudence, Anna, and the children filed by on their way to the church. He would not be attending; he never did. Prudence returned the greeting with a nod.

The church was filled with the continuously kind, sad eyes that gazed at the Lenhart family. It was too painful for Prudence, for she knew the darkness in her heart.

The marriage had been a duty, to her parents, to her community, to her wounded pride. It was a duty that was not without its comforts and joys, but a duty nonetheless. She felt guilty that her mind was not constantly filled with Emil's memory; it wandered to and fro with a lightness that she had forgotten was hers.

She touched the hand of each child tenderly and leaned towards Anna, whispering, "Take them home and let them play. I need to be alone for a while. I'll be home before supper."

It was halfway through the sermon when she excused herself. Only half of the congregation forgave the behavior of the unscheduled exit.

Prudence walked in the direction of her parents' farm, but turned off the road just before and headed into the woods. Karl followed at a safe distance, knowing precisely where she was headed. It was an abandoned fur-trapper's shed, long forgotten by everyone else. They had discovered it on an adventure interrupted by rain when they were nine years old and had vowed never to show the place to anyone. Perhaps others knew, but there was no evidence indicating that. Karl had broken that promise once, with Mercedes early in their courtship. He never returned, nor did he want to. Prudence had broken her vow precisely five times, once with each of her children, when they would be too young to remember.

Prudence broke into a run once she reached the Indian burial mound, framed by three birch trees on either side. The shed lay just beyond the mound. She pushed the door open and threw herself down on the tatter of the bed frame. It wasn't as disgusting as it could have been since she had been there only two months before to have her private celebration with the baby after the spring thaw made it possible.

Finally, she could cry a guilty cry for feeling alive. The hot tears of relief soaked the ragged pallet. The guilt of not feeling sufficient grief escaped in great gasps and hiccoughs. She pounded her fists on the bed frame and then on her chest.

The door creaked, betraying Karl's presence. She looked up at him and ran to his arms. She sobbed as he endeavored to act as an "extra brother." He sought refuge in that role when she used to drop her hints, her endearing attempts to vamp him years earlier. He would act as the extra brother when other young men were near. Later, he would tap into that caring persona when she'd look worn with her family cares.

Slowly, she gathered herself together, broke free of his embrace, and talked to the shelves on the opposite wall, "I have three hours before the moral repercussions of what I'm about to say sink in."

An audible breath was his only response, but his confusion was clear.

She turned towards him but looked only at her own hands. "I'll serve it up anyway you like it, right here, right now. This will be our only chance."

"Pru, you don't have to..."

"No, I *do* have to. It's all I've thought about since...since that day. Isn't that awful? Through the funeral, through church services, through caring for Emil's children, I've been thinking about you instead."

"It's not that I don't want to, it's ..."

She interrupted him again. "If you want me to seduce you, I will seduce you. If you want me to resist, I will resist you. If you want me to be shy, I'll be as innocent as the day we met. If you want me to tell you what to do, I'll give you plenty of instruction. If you want me to respond to every touch, all I need is the chance. Just want me. Want me enough to tell me so. Want me enough to do something about it."

***

It was one day after the first anniversary of Emil Lenhart's burial that Karl walked up the front path of the Lenhart household, carrying the early blooms that he had picked from the gardens in the Catholic cemetery at the other end of town. Although it was a Wednesday, the door to his workshop had a sign nailed to it: **GONE COURTING.**

He was in his Sunday best now that he had Sunday best. He had started taking his mother to church a little less than a year ago. After so many years of resisting such conformity, he only answer was "Out of gratitude" to those who inquired as to why.

***

Perhaps Karl wasn't the restless man everyone always thought he was. He had been so helpful offering to teach her oldest boy a trade, perhaps because he missed his own son. Of course, they had been friends for years. Surely, a widow with six children couldn't possibly have had so much money that she'd be worth marrying for money.

She'd been such a rock for her children too. And the baby, so tiny for a full term baby, must have been conceived just before his father left for Madison. Poor thing, born without ever knowing his father! How she fretted about that baby!

About the author:
Jean Tschohl Quinn started out as a Wisconsinite, played at being a Virginian after college, pretended to be an Illinoisan for a while, is begrudgingly becoming a Californian but prefers to be

considered a world citizen.

A mathematician by degree, a musician by choice, a mom by—-well, we all know the usual way one gets to be a mom—stories started attacking from out of the blue in November of '06. She can't make them stop, so she thought she'd try sharing them. She lives with her husband, three teen-aged daughters, two dogs and several hundred redwood trees.

REMORSE
©2008 by DS Winkle

As she looked at him lying in the hospital bed, she was filled with the most immense sense of loss she had ever felt. How did this come to be? This morning she had gotten out of bed determined to tell her husband that things were going to change. She was going to tell him that she would stop drinking. She had told him this many times before, but this time was for real. Chester was getting too old to have to keep working at the mill. His friends had retired many years ago, but Chester said he kept working because it kept him young. Etta knew, however, Chester would have liked nothing more than to punch out of the old factory for the last time, grab his fishing pole and spend the rest of his years reeling in bass on Lake Palomey.

Etta first saw Chester walking down the steps of Montgomery High School some fifty years ago. From the moment they spoke, he said he knew she was the woman he'd be with for the rest of his life. Those who knew them marveled at how there was never an argument or so much as a disagreement between the two for the many years of their marriage. Even when it was discovered that Etta could not bear children, Chester chalked it up to God's will and continued to hold Etta's hand at the movies, buy her flowers for her birthday and kiss her hello every day after coming home from work.

Now seeing Chester hooked up to so many machines, Etta could not convince herself of the reality of the situation. The doctors had told Etta things didn't look good, but as long as the beeping was strong and steady, Etta knew Chester would pull through. It was ironic that Chester had been working so hard to pay Etta's medical bills, and now it was he who needed her support.

In all the years where Etta had been drinking, Chester never once raised his voice. When Etta would yell and scream and cry, Chester understood it was just the devil's juice making his beloved behave that way. He would wait until she got it out of her system, and the next day he would let her sleep until she came back to herself. And most of the time she did.

Chester was always such a docile man. Etta's friends all told her how lucky she was to have a husband who never raised his hand to her. He was kind and good, and his only goal in life was to provide for his wife. Etta was the one who had dreams. She wanted to move to the big city and live in a big house with white columns. She wanted to wear those dresses she saw in the magazines and sip lemonade in the garden. Forty years later, however, Etta was still living in Brownsboro and, instead of sipping lemonade, she was chasing her expensive prescription pills with a couple shots of whiskey.

Etta doesn't really remember what came first, the pills or the liquor. It was more than ten years ago that Chester had found her on the bathroom floor and rushed her to the hospital. She had been bleeding from her wrists. After that she started seeing the head doctor every week. It took many months for the doctor to find the pills that worked, but one day Etta woke up and for the first time in a long while didn't feel like crying. The pills helped in that she never again found herself on the bathroom floor, but they didn't always replace the Jim Beam.

Chester's overtime paid for the pills. Unfortunately, his working on the weekends and late into the night left Etta at home alone with her demons, and it wasn't until it got real bad that Chester took notice of his wife's habit. Instead of reprimanding Etta, Chester held her and prayed to the Lord to heal his wife's sickness. Many times it seemed as though his prayers were working, but then some nights he would again find her sleeping on the couch with an empty bottle beside her, and he would put her to bed.

However, last night was different. Chester came home early

because he was tired, and he wanted to spend some time with his wife. Although Etta had not been drinking when Chester got home, when she saw him come through the door, something inside her snapped. She started screaming and cursing and telling Chester she wanted more out of life. She told him she didn't want to live in Brownsboro anymore. She told him she wanted a new house and her own car. She told him their house was a rundown shack and they had nothing to show for their years together. No children. No money. No future.

And then Etta said to Chester the last words she would ever say to him. "You failed me."

After Etta spoke these words, Chester looked at her for a long time and was silent. His face reflected the heartache of a man who had himself been missing happiness but who did not know it until now. Chester took his jacket out of the coat closet, walked down the hall and out the front door.

It took Etta a few minutes to regain herself and realize what she had said. She ran outside and saw that Chester had taken the car, so she started walking down the four-mile road to town. It was just getting dark and, because it was dinner time, not many cars passed her. Those who knew her asked if she needed a lift, but she declined. She walked briskly and made it to town in under an hour. She walked past Lenny's Diner and saw only two tables occupied by families she did not know. There were two men sitting at the counter, neither of which was Chester. Etta continued down to the bowling alley, but it was completely quiet; the first patrons most likely not showing up for another hour. Etta searched up and down Main Street for any sign of Chester's car, but saw nothing.

Etta turned the corner and saw Cal's Bar. She approached it slowly and decided she should stop in and see whether any of Chester's old friends from the mill were there and had seen him. Cal told her he hadn't seen Chester in quite some time and asked whether she wanted a drink. Etta said she'd like a coke, and Cal served her one.

Much time passed, and it became apparent to Etta that Chester was not coming into Cal's tonight. Her nerves were on edge. She didn't know how much of it was due to the words she had said to her husband and how much of it was due to the six cokes she had downed since waiting for him to come through the door. When Cal asked if she wanted another refill, she told him he better make it a Jack and coke this time. By the time Cal told her it was last call, Etta felt more relaxed and accepted his offer to drive her home after he closed up.

As Cal and Etta were approaching her house, she noticed the sheriff's car out front. When she got out of the car, Sheriff Daniels put his arm on her shoulder and told her Chester had been in a bad accident and was at the county hospital. He told Etta to get in his car, and he would drive her there.

Etta does not remember the forty-five-minute drive to the hospital. Nor does she remember all the details the doctors told her about Chester's injuries or how she finally got to the room where Chester was lying hooked up to all those machines, including the one making the loud beeping sounds. All she knew now was she had to be strong for him. For the man who had been strong for her these last fifty-some years; for the man lying unconscious in front of her, with machines helping him breathe.

Etta started by telling Chester she didn't mean what she said. She told him it was the drinking that made her say crazy things and even though she had been drinking a bit that night, she would never touch another drop. She told him she loved him and couldn't live without him. She told him she knew no other man would put up with her. She told him he was a good man and he deserved a better wife. She promised him she would change. She would be happy, and she wouldn't need the pills. He wouldn't have to keep working such long hours. She would take care of him.

As she recited these words, she began to believe them herself. She would stop drinking and be grateful for what she had: a good home and a loving husband. She would never again want for something she didn't have. She would stop worrying so much about herself and think of others. She would spend their money on groceries instead of liquor, and she would cook Chester his favorite meal: fried catfish with greens and cornbread. Chester could spend the days fishing with his friends and come home to a loving wife in the evenings.

She felt strong and confident and for the first time in a long while she felt at peace. She looked at her husband lying on the bed and smiled. She did not even notice that the beeping had stopped.

About the author:

DS Winkle has lived in Chicago most of her life. She works in Human Resources for a large financial institution and has just recently begun to write short stories. She and her husband love traveling, hiking and baseball. DS believes interactions between people are what make life interesting, and the key to happiness is not to take oneself too seriously. "Remorse" is her first published work, and she hopes to dedicate more time for writing in the future

SOUTHERN GIRL
2008 by Philip Loyd

"Well, at least she's no damn Yankee," said Mother, and that was the closest thing to a compliment I could have expected. "That girl you...while you were at Princeton, the one with the...with the nose, you know, the..."

"The Jewish girl," I said.

Mother stopped breathing.

"Don't you use that tone with me," she said. "This new girl, she's not...she's not..."

"No Mother, she's not Jewish."

She started breathing again.

"She's a Southern girl," I said.

"Watch your mouth," said my Mother, pointing her fork at me. "You watch your manners in my house."

I had to give Mother the benefit of the doubt. Before lunch today, she didn't even know I had a girlfriend, much less that I was engaged.

My girlfriend, my fiancé, I had known for only three months now. I met her in Houston. As far as I was concerned, she was as much a Southerner as any belle from Savannah or debutante from New Orleans. But Mother didn't regard Texans as Southerners. Mother believed all ladies west of the Sabine River crowned their curtilage with cactus roses, and that all men moussed their hair with motor oil.

"Now, you know my problem with that last girl was not that she was Jewish," said Mother, "or that she was a Yankee."

"Yes, Mother."

"I mean, not for the sake of being Jewish or being a Yankee, per say. But go ahead and tell me how I was wrong about her. "

"You were right about her, Mother."

"Tell me how I didn't warn you about her."

"You warned me about her, Mother."

"It's not that I want to gloat. God forbid I should want to see you happy. But, like I've told you a thousand times before, you need—"

"A Southern girl."

"So, tell me about this new girl," said Mother. Mother loved being right almost as much as she loved sounding magnanimous.

"Well, like I said, she's a Southern girl," and thinking about Mary made my eyes light up. "You're just going to fall in love with her."

Mother grunted.

"She's everything that's splendid about a Southern girl. She has big beautiful brown eyes, dewy skin that glistens, pouty lips, a loving smile, and long, straight hair that falls down past her shoulders to her waist."

"I see," said Mother.

"And with Mary, family means everything."

"You don't say. Is she from a large family?"

"Eight sisters, six brothers."

"Oh my, that is a healthy family. And what does her father do?"

"He's a doctor."

"What's his specialty?"

"He's a GP."

"I didn't know there were any old country doctors still around," said Mother.

"He even makes house calls."

"You don't say. And her mother?"

"Where do you think Mary gets her exquisite eyes? She's the most beautiful elderly woman I've ever met," I said, "next to you."

"*Mature* woman," said Mother, and I think she actually blushed. "I suppose you two are already living together, like you did with that one from New York?"

"Not a chance," I said. "Mary wouldn't have it. As far as things like that go, she says 'I don't' until we both say 'I do'."

"Impressive," said Mother. Mother was rarely impressed.

I grabbed Mother by her hand. I could see she was a bit startled by this. No one ever grabbed Mother by her hand.

"I have to tell you, Mother," I said, "Mary, her whole family, there is something so quaint about them, it's almost as if they were from another time and place. It's just like the stories you always tell me, about how it was growing up with Grandma and Grandpa. There is something about her that reminds me of, well, of you."

Mother had never heard me talk this way before.

"Mary is nothing like any of the girls I've dated before, nothing like women today at all. She doesn't drink, doesn't smoke, doesn't go out dancing all night, doesn't wear scant clothing, isn't a flirt; hell, she never even had a steady boyfriend before me. The only beau she ever had was when she was fifteen and they only had two dates and they never even left her house.

"And now this, you're just not going to believe," I said. Mother almost looked frightened. "We've had a dozen dates altogether, and that's counting the times I've been to her house. Never, not once, have we been alone. Either her father or her mother or her grandmother has always been there to chaperone. I'm not kidding. That's how old-fashioned she is."

"My word," said Mother. "Sounds like someone straight out of a Herbert Sass novel." She swallowed hard. "Sounds like your father and I."

"I know."

"So," said Mother, "when do I get to meet this future daughter-in-law of mine, this *Southern* girl?" She touched my hand and smiled.

"Well, I said, "how about right now?"

"Excuse me?"

"She's just outside, in the car. I'll go and get her."

"Here, she's here now?" said Mother, and she began searching for a mirror. "But I don't even have my face on." Absent a mirror, she set to fixing her hair by her reflection in the silver tea set. I hadn't seen Mother this out of sorts since President Clinton came to console her at my father's funeral.

I gave Mother the few extra moments I knew she'd want, and even knocked first.

"Come in," she said.

I opened the door. Mother was standing stiff as a board, smiling wide with starched hair and the scent of freshly sprayed perfume all around. It was the biggest smile I ever saw her make, and it lasted all of one second. At two seconds, the arch in her back gave way and her shoulders slumped forward. In the third second, all the color in her face washed away and she was as white as a ghost.

At least she looked bleached white, especially in contrast to Mary, who wrapped her caramel-colored arms around Mother, hugging her like she was family already, saying *"Mamá, finalmente nos conocemos, aunque parece que ya te conociera."*

Mother should be happy, I thought. Mary—Maria—reminds me of her in so many ways. She is the very definition of a Southern girl: a natural-born beauty; ladylike in manner and style; devoted to hard work; dedicated to family; and as old-fashioned as they come. She is from the small town of Cardenas in southern Mexico.

And oh yes, one thing Mary most certainly is not: she's no damn Yankee.

About the author:

Philip Loyd resides in Houston Texas and is the author of 37 short stories. His work including essays, poetry, and book reviews has appeared in 83 publications in 7 countries with one story even produced for radio in Australia. Included in his numerous awards is the Hemingway Center Short Story Prize.

BENEATH THE MAKEUP
2008 by Ruth Wire

I am an actor. I am not a child molester. But they say I am. They took me away from Ellen, my wife, and Laila, my daughter, and put me in the perverts' special ward at Atascadero. Do you know what they do to you there? It's called "aversion therapy." They rid your mind of any thoughts of your particular perversion, but I had none. I'd never touched any child before.

Laila was thirteen. I've never had the urge to do unspeakable things to little girls. But I had to undergo the same treatment as the inmates I lived with. One guy, a fat slob, admitted he couldn't wait to get out. He had fantasies that made me sick. In the cell we shared, he always described with nostalgia the children he'd molested, until I couldn't stand it anymore. I told him to shut the hell up, the sick bastard.

I knew I, Jon Bernard Ditmar, a first-time offender, was with terrible people, in a horrible place, being treated for the one wrong thing I'd ever done. But they kept me there for three years. They hacked away at my personality. I felt chopped to pieces. I found myself admitting things I hadn't done—or couldn't do.

One grey day, I really believed I was as weird as they said I was, and found myself saying things to satisfy them. I'd shrunk physically to a bony ghost of myself. I looked ten-years older than I was, and I realized that this one mistake I'd made had ruined all my hopes for the future. My one wish was to get out of there, so I played along, and made myself believe I was a sexual monster.

My role in the last play before Laila told her mother about us was Gollum in a production of *The Hobbit. Oh my precious, how I covet thee.*

Before that, I was a valuable member of a community theatre group, a thirty-something guy with ordinary looks. The kind of guy who, as our producer Marla said, delivers the paper from his bicycle. I was, in Marla's eyes, normal as apple pie and just as forgettable. However, as a standard fit-all-types actor I was perfect. The theatre found many useful roles for me, mainly in comedies. As a carpenter, I gave hours of time to set building. The kids loved me and I helped out with children's classes.

Oh shit. Why do I remind myself of these things? I can never work with children again. I can't go near a playground or be a teacher. I move pianos for a living these days.

I don't know what happened with Ellen. We loved each other when we married. I never wanted anybody else. Ellen was going for her master's degree in English and taking a lot of classes. I was spending a lot of time at the theatre. You know how it was...we drifted apart.

But I still had Laila, my precious daughter. She loved me as all the children did. I made her laugh. Laila grew from a curly headed toddler into a pretty pre-teen before I knew it. I would always tell her a bedtime story, even when she was thirteen.

When I took on the part of the Gollum, something happened to me. First of all, here was an interesting role, not my usual innocent good-guy-can't-think-of-wrong type. The Gollum was frustrated. And I found myself frustrated. Ellen looked past me—or through me—at home. It hurt. I tried to go by the psych books, to stir up our sexual relationship, but it felt wrong. She must have felt it too because she looked amused.

Even roses on Valentine's Day didn't help. It was a clumsy attempt, but I didn't want to lose Ellen. Ellen smiled thinly and gave me a peck on the cheek, so I threw myself into the characterization of the Gollum, and sulked.

At bedtime, I'd tell Laila of my thwarted attempts at relieving frustration by becoming the Gollum, who, in Tolkien's books, is the ultimate betrayer. He lusts after the Ring and will do anything to get it: lie, cheat, kill. He splits into two people: *Smeagol*, who is the restraining hand, and *Gollum*, a loathsome toad-like creature, who eats things picked out of the mud and slithers over rocks looking for the Ring he lost, with his desires out in the open.

They won't give it to me, my precious! I'll do anything it get it back, but Smeagol won't let Gollum have what he wants. But he wants it. He needs it. I am sad for poor Gollum.

Laila loved me playing Gollum/Smeagol. She liked it when I got on all fours on the bed and pretended to be half-frog and splayed myself on top of her on the covers, clutching the pillows, my fingers spread like a gecko.

I feel something here, my precious. What can it be? Oh, it's my lady's curls. What wondrous curls. Now where is that Ring? Is it here? Or here? Maybe under the covers! Here it is! Now I have it and I won't give it back. It's mine, precious, mine, all mine!

I can't tell you when playing became real. Laila laughed at my silliness at first. She laughed when I first touched her breasts. Then she looked scared because my hand didn't stop. I explored her like the Gollum, whispering and hissing, gently, very gently.

My bedtime stories became a nightly adventure while Ellen hit the books downstairs. I shed tears at the discovery of my daughter's sweet body. She was becoming more beautiful than my wife without the coldness I felt in Ellen.

Laila held me in her arms and said sadly, "Don't cry, Daddy. It's all right. It really is."

Gollum-like, I made her my accomplice. "Nice Laila, pretty Laila. This is our special secret, yesss?"

"I love you, Daddy."

Somebody loved me. My own precious child. I swear I could never hurt that beautiful being. But they say I did.

One night, Laila said, "I have to tell Mommy."

I felt suddenly cold. "Why?"

Laila's forehead wrinkled with anxiety. "Mommy keeps asking me what we do up here at bedtime."

I couldn't look at my child. I had used her because I wanted her mother. A sour taste rose from my stomach. "What will you tell her, darling?"

"That you touch me. That you—I know that other thing isn't right."

I sat with my head bent to my knees. "It's okay, Laila. You have to. I understand. I'm so sorry."

We both began to cry.

***

Police sirens screeched to a stop at our house the next day, while the silent, outraged Ellen opened the door for them. They found me in my bathrobe, drinking coffee.

"Mr. Ditmar?" asked the arresting officer in a neutral voice, charging me with molestation of a minor, officially making something dirty out of our relationship. Laila sobbed, clinging to Ellen, while they put handcuffs on me.

The cops smirked when I said, "Have I hurt you, Laila?"

"No! No! But I had to tell, Daddy."

My poor Laila. That is what confused me so much. I was a weak man. I couldn't reach Ellen, couldn't excuse myself, couldn't look into her eyes. She'd turned to stone.

Laila wrung her hands. "What will happen to you, Daddy?"

I was as if dead. I couldn't move. The sun was gone from my world. Yet, I could watch myself from a distance, so I said calmly, "What happened to the Gollum, I guess."

"He disappeared."

Taking refuge in acting, I intoned, "Banishment. Dishonor. Disgrace."

Laila threw herself into my arms. "Don't go away!"

Stroking her hair, I said, "I may have to."

"Will I see you again?"

"I don't know." I could barely say the next. "Do you want to?"

"Oh, Daddy!" Laila clung to me in desperation. "What did I do to you?"

Of course, the question should have been, "What did you do to me?" That will come later as Laila matures. I know all about it now. It's been pounded into my head. What power fathers have over their daughters.

I moved a piano for Marla the other day. She looked shocked at my appearance. I guess I've lost a lot of weight, and I've got prison pallor. She had no smart remarks, but it was in her eyes. *How could you do such a thing?* What I did is beyond awful for someone like Marla, but she did ask for my help today, maybe just out of curiosity.

What does a monster look like? I'm still Jon Bernard Ditmar. I'm not a scumbag. I'm a very good actor, and from what I've been through, I understand pain and guilt and can use it to create roles. I've never been sexual with any child except Laila, and that happened, it seems to me, as a natural consequence of our emotional intimacy.

Laila's mind has been poisoned by Ellen. She won't see me, and the authorities believe I'm like those other guys. But it's not in my constitution. *They* think about kids all day. Still, being around guys like that for so long, I have a weariness a forty-something shouldn't have. I have been to the grave and returned.

The thing is, how am I going to spend the rest of my life?

About the author:

Ruth has been writing since age 11, when her girlfriend and she cut their fingers and mingled blood, vowing to become writers. Her friend became a social worker and Ruth became a nurse.

Ruth took up writing again after she had two children. Her poetry has been published in *Blue Satellite, Beyond Baroque Anthology, American Journal of Nursing, The Rag, Four Poets, New Venice Poets, Convergence, Mad Poets, 2000, HayWire Anthology*, and *42 Grandmothers*.

Ruth taught "Letting Poetry Happen" for the Young Writers in the Rogue Valley. She won the Bultman Award for a one-act play in 1980, which was produced by Loyola University, New Orleans. Most of her plays have been produced in Ashland, OR. She ran two theatres in the 1980's and now works for Ashland Community Theatre.

She has also won two awards on one screenplay, and runs HayWire Writers' Workshop, where they've released an anthology of their work.